Preparing
Polishing
Perfecting
Emma

BDSM Training School Parts 4-6

LEXIE RENARD
BDSM EROTICA

Welcome to my perverted little world, where sexy people love to play with sensations of pleasure, pain, submission and control. Want more? Get on the email list for a free story! www.LexieRenard.com

lexie.renard@gmail.com   **@lexierenard**

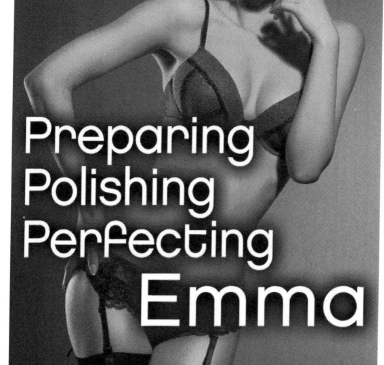

Preparing
Polishing
Perfecting
Emma

BDSM Training School Parts 4 - 6

LEXIE RENARD
BDSM EROTICA

***

Table of Contents

***

Preparing Emma
(BDSM Training School Book #4)

*** THE BDSM ACADEMY ***

The BDSM Academy is rarely spoken of beyond a whisper. But if you beg the owners, organizers, and Dominants of the most respected dungeons, they may pass your name along for consideration.

Seven of the most respected Dominants and Dominatrixes in the city banded together to create an informal program where submissives could learn as much as they wanted about the BDSM world in a safe environment.

They were tired of seeing newcomers so desperate for the experience that they allowed less than reputable "Masters" and "Mistresses" to pick them up. With no experience, guidance, or mentorship, it was far too easy for abusive and manipulative people to take advantage of them.

In order to sign up for the BDSM Academy, applicants must commit to a thirty-day, twenty-four-seven submissive lifestyle, giving themselves completely to the whims of their Master or Mistress. This will ensure that they are extremely serious, and allow them to completely fall into the submissive headspace, learn about the lifestyle, and discover what they really wanted for themselves.

One can only determine what one truly needs from a Dominant if one has been dominated.

*** THE DECISION ***

The next thirty days of my life were depending on the luck of the draw.

I had been extremely fortunate over the past several months, as there have either been too few submissives for the Masters and Mistresses interested, or on two occasions I was assigned submissives who were only interested in servitude, obedience, and punishment, with absolutely no sexual element to our play.

That suited me just fine. Just six months ago my submissive sweetheart, whom I had thought had been the love of my life, suddenly left town for a singing gig on a cruise ship. I hadn't even known that that was something she was interested in. But it seemed more that she was running away from me, then running to a new career.

I had foolishly let myself trust her, opening up and actually letting her see the real me. I could never allow that to happen again.

Yet here I was ready to welcome a submissive into my home for a month, to train them, educate them, and help them become the best sub possible during this time.

I couldn't be around the other Dominants joking and laughing while they went through the files as the submissives waited in another room. Leaving Jeremy's huge house by the back door, I snuck out to the secondary parking area. Maybe if I sat in my car for a bit and listened to some loud music it would clear my head.

I was suddenly glad I had brought the car instead of my bike. Taking a terrified submissive home on a motorcycle might frighten them a bit too much.

As I was digging for my keys, I saw a girl sitting on a rock a few feet away. When I got closer, I saw that she was studying her shaking hands.

"Excuse me, are you okay?"

She looked up at me, startled, then relaxed as she seemed to recognize me. "Oh, hi. You're Master Darren, aren't you?"

"Yes. Are you one of the submissives for the selection meeting?"

I was desperately hoping that she'd say she wasn't. Maybe she was just a server, or other temporary party staff. Her huge almond eyes were so expressive, lighting up a picture-perfect beautiful face. She was petite, with those narrow shoulders and regal neckline clearing stating she had once taken ballet. Her short blonde hair was a flirty little halo around her gorgeous face.

She was absolutely everything I was looking for in a submissive physically, at the time when I was seriously trying not to look at all.

"Yes," she almost whispered. "But now that I'm here, I'm not quite as sure."

I sat down beside her on the stone wall surrounding the parking lot, keeping a little distance between us. Some women are a bit nervous around me since I'm such a big guy, but this tiny girl seemed to have no fear at all now that she knew my name.

"I'm Emma," she said, holding out her hand for me to gently shake.

"It's nice to meet you. So, you were sure about the program, and now you're having doubts?"

"Yeah." The golden glow of the streetlamp made her soft blush absolutely adorable. "Um, a lot of people are into BDSM for the bondage and rules and all of the technical stuff. I don't know a lot about that side of it."

"You're here to learn. That's okay." Stopping my hand from reaching out to hold hers, I asked, "What side of it do you like? What draws you to it?"

Looking up at me, she seemed to think for a second before blurting, "The sex. I've only had truly hot sex once in my life, and I was tied up and dominated, and I've been hoping to find that again, but as a regular thing."

"You gave permission to be tied up?"

"Yes," she laughed lightly, realizing I was already checking in. "Last year the guy I was seeing wanted to get a bit wild, and I played along just as an experiment. It was amazing. But then he got transferred out of town, and I've been reading up on this stuff, and now…"

"You're nervous about giving in to it entirely for a whole month."

"Exactly."

"But you know that your dominant will be checking in with you, making sure you're learning what you need, getting what you want."

"The thing I need most is sex," she blurted, looking instantly horrified.

I chuckled, trying to keep the mood light. "There's nothing wrong with that. The human animal craves sex. It's a basic need."

"But what if I'm paired with someone I don't click with?"

I couldn't help noticing that she was checking out my arms and chest, barely covered by my tight black t-shirt. Some of the dominants went for the whole fancy leather vibe, but I was a guy who fixed cars, rode a motorbike and wore jeans. Dressing up didn't suit me.

"Well, if you don't click with the dominant in that way, then you'll be learning more about the other side of the lifestyle – service and patience and obedience."

"Will that work without the sex?"

"Of course. It will set you up with a foundation of knowledge that you can you when you find the right person at the right time."

"Why are you here?" she asked suddenly. "What are you looking for in a submissive?"

"I…" How honest should I be, I thought. "I had a harsh experience with a sub six months ago. Bad breakup. So now I'm actually looking to teach more of the technical side. I don't know if I'm ready for anything physical yet."

"Damn," she said saucily. "I was just warming up to you."

My low chuckle seemed to amuse her. "You'd likely be learning far more about bondage than you're ready for."

"I liked it when my hands were tied that one time. It was trippy. But I knew that I could have pulled harder and gotten out."

"And what if you couldn't?"

She shrugged. "I don't know. I guess I'd learn what the appeal was, or that I wasn't really into it." Those piercing eyes examined mine. "Hearing the way you seem to like it, it sounds more exciting instead of scary."

"I know I am just some weirdo in a parking lot, but can I show you?" I knew I shouldn't be doing this, treating a random girl in a parking lot as my submissive. But I loved teaching people new things.

"Okay."

"Stand up."

We stood facing each other, and I stayed perfectly still for a few moments until she became a little anxious. Then I grabbed her wrists, pinning them behind her back, yanking her toward me.

Although I was watching her eyes and shoulders for any sign of distress, ready to release her in a heartbeat, I was instantly overcome by her soft scent. The tiniest breath of vanilla mint or something, washing over me. Her energy was so delicate, it was like she was a fairy. Not of this world.

She tried to be still, but wiggled a little. "You're mine now. How does that make you feel?" I growled.

"I don't know," she said honestly. Emma wasn't scared, just off guard. Off kilter. Her arms instinctively kept shifting position, but I had her held tightly.

"Do you see how this feels? Is your heart racing? Do you see how you're now my toy? That is what bondage does. It lowers the walls. It makes everything clear."

She became still, looking up at me strangely. Her eyes were more intense than I had expected.

"When you're captured, it makes the release feel more interesting," I said, letting go of her and starting to step back.

The second her hands were free she lunged at me, wrapping her arms around my neck and pulling my lips down to hers.

Every part of her overwhelmed me completely, and I adored that she was so aggressive. Her soft lips pressed into mine with a fire I would never have expected. My hands circled her waist before I could stop them, pulling her whole body in tight. I needed her. I needed to please her, to make her squeal in bliss...

She jumped back, her hands flying to cover her face. "Oh my God – I'm so sorry. I just..."

I took a deep, slow breath to pull myself together. "If you were my submissive, touching your Master without permission would mean being put over my knee for a rough spanking."

Watching her eyes carefully, I could see that the idea of me manhandling her and smacking her little ass thrilled her completely.

"Would you really do that?" she asked softly, stepping closer again and fluttering those long lashes. "Would you really give me a spanking? Would you smack me until I squeal?"

My hands gripped her pert ass, pulling her against me again roughly. "Emma, I would discipline you until you were the most patient, dedicated, controlled submissive you could possibly imagine."

"What about when it's time to lose control?"

We stared at each other, her hands pressing slowly up my chest. Her eyes were blazing, and I could barely tear my gaze away except to notice her soft, pouty lips parting slightly, her pink tongue darting between them.

The air became hot and thick between us. It was like a game of chicken, whoever moved first would be the one making the decision. But we lunged at the same time, kissing each other so hard it was probably dangerous.

I tried to stop my hands from groping her breasts through her dress, cupping her firm ass. But she was caressing me everywhere, her delicate hands under my shirt already.

"You're so hot," she breathed, as I nibbled her bottom lip, trying to find some self-control.

"Emma, we shouldn't…"

Her lightning-quick hands were unfastening my belt, my jeans, pulling my cock out right here in the back parking lot.

"Holy shit," she gasped, her fingers stroking me firmly, exploring my skin. I hadn't been touched by a woman in months, and was harder than I could believe. "You're huge," she breathed, examining me as if she were afraid of it.

Grabbing her by the waist, I threw her up on the hood of my car, spreading her silky thighs, running my hands up between them. My fingertips glided over the gusset of her panties. She was soaked, the fabric clinging to her bare pussy lips.

"Yes," she breathed, wrapping her legs around me and drawing me closer.

Pulling her panties aside, she grabbed my shaft, rubbing it against her wet lips. For a girl this pretty and perfect to be so bold, so wanton, I was losing all control.

"Are you sure?"

"Yes," she moaned, pulling me in. Pressing into her

softness a few inches, I couldn't believe the sensation of her warm, wet passage drawing me in.

Grabbing her wrists behind her back again, I gazed into her eyes. "You understand safewords?"

"Green, yellow, red."

"You'll speak up immediately if this is too much?"

"Yes… Sir."

Oh fuck. Gripping her tightly, I leaned her back against the cold metal as I plunged inside the tightest, most luscious pussy I'd ever felt in my life. She was so tight I could only work myself inside her about four inches, but it didn't matter. My careful strokes were driving us both insane as I gently stretched her a tiny bit more.

Reaching into her sopping panties, I lightly skimmed my thumb over her clit. She squealed, but my lips met hers again to silence her. The hot, wet sounds of our fucking rang through the parking lot, along with her sexy moaning.

"I'll teach you to be silent if you're mine."

A shudder ran through her that I could actually feel. "Make me yours."

Bringing my lips to her ear, I murmured, "I'd tie you in my bed for days. I'd make you come so many times you couldn't see. I'd fuck that pretty mouth every morning." I've never spoken like this to anyone, and had no idea what was coming over me.

"Yes," she cried, her hips trembling as I thrust as deeply as her tight little cunt allowed. "Please, make me your slave girl."

She rocked against me desperately, and I glanced down for a glimpse of her wet, pink pussy lips wrapped around my huge cock. The fact that I was actually too big for her aroused me even more.

"I'd train your tight pussy to take it all," I growled, and she looked up at me, panting and nodding. Fucking her faster, swirling my thumb over her clit, I could feel that she was right on the edge. Every stroke was building the heat between us, and I actually felt like I might explode from the intensity of her hot body against mine.

"Come," I ordered, my dark, commanding tone ringing through the air.

Emma suddenly became silent, quivering and limp. Then she screamed, her body shaking, rocking against me as I pounded into her a little deeper. Her hot, drenched pussy clenched around me as I shook with her, kissing her violently as I filled her completely with thick ropes of cum. I'd never felt anything so utterly perfect in my life.

The second I released her, her arms flew around me again as she laid back, pulling me with her. I took a few more leisurely strokes into her wetness, then pulled out, letting our juices drip along the metal hood.

Exploding in laughter, she choked, "Some poor guy is going to find a helluva mess on his car."

"It's mine," I said, kissing down her throat, pulling her dress down to lick her nipple. Then I came to my senses. "We have to go."

Quickly putting ourselves back together, I wasn't sure what to say. Then she turned to me. "Can you pick which submissive you end up with?"

"There is a hierarchy of choosing. But I can see what I can do."

"I want you to take me."

I couldn't help laughing. "I thought I just did."

She giggled, giving my bicep a playful swat. In a flash I had both of her hands over her head, pulling her up so that she was almost on her toes.

"You'll be disciplined very strictly, little girl."

"Yes, Sir," she said sweetly. "But I think I'll understand it better if we enjoy the same… release afterward."

I was already helplessly addicted to her. How the hell could I teach her discipline if I couldn't control myself? It was ridiculous. But it was too late now.

Releasing her arms, she grabbed her purse from where she had dropped it on the stone wall. "I'm going to run to the washroom to clean up, and I'll see you in there." She cocked her head, grinning. "Sir." She stretched up to give me a swift kiss, then she was gone.

Walking slowly toward the building, I knew that I was beyond hooked. And that although Master Jeremy would likely give me the first pick of submissives, given the circumstances, he would also be laughing at me for several weeks.

*** HOPING ***

My hands were shaking as I used the washroom, then cleaned myself up as well as I could. The girl staring back at me in the mirror looked stunned, rumpled and freshly fucked. Thank goodness this haircut looked cuter the more it was messed up. But the smile that reflected back at me was the first genuine happiness I'd felt in ages.

How could I fuck some stranger in the parking lot? But he wasn't a stranger. He was the one. The man I'd been searching for. The one who was going to teach me.

I couldn't believe this was happening. One moment I was talking myself into coming here and giving myself to a Master for a month to learn everything I could, the next minute I was in the parking lot trying to decide whether it was right.

The tone of his voice when he gave me the order to climax... I quivered just thinking about it. The thought of obeying that sound for the next month unraveled me.

Now I was certain. This was my Master. This was the man who was going to teach me what I wanted to know. Another shudder ran through me when I realized he would be taking me as often as he wanted. That couldn't have been a one-time thing. The heat between us was intoxicating. If he didn't choose me, or if someone else did, I didn't know what I'd do.

Joining the rest of the submissives in the lounge, I sat quietly at the end of a sofa. There was a huge mirror across one wall that was obviously one-way glass. I wasn't sure how the system worked, but the Dominants were likely going through our files, matching up who wanted to teach with who wanted to learn.

I did want to learn. The whole BDSM lifestyle had a bit of the dark, dangerous vibe I was looking for right now. But I was a hands on sort of learner. Books and videos didn't really interest me. I needed someone to teach me in person. Even though a whole month was a bit of a strange gamble. But if Darren was my Master, I knew I'd learn so much. Hopefully I could help him loosen up and let go a little too.

*** Choosing Emma ***

The Dominants were all perusing the files, deciding as a group who should be paired with who. Since Jeremy had decided to keep his new submissive Sierra, he was helping everyone instead of trying to find someone for himself.

I sidled over to him. "Hey, Jeremy, congrats on the new sub. I hear that things are working out well."

He gave me a grin I hadn't seen from him in ages. "Yeah. She's... she's amazing."

Clapping him on the back, I said, "I'm really happy for you, man."

"Thanks." He nodded toward the mirror. "Anyone you might click with?"

I leaned closer, lowering my voice. "Yes. In fact, we've already clicked."

He gave me a curious look but didn't press further. "Who is she?"

"Emma."

Jeremy nodded, walking over to Miranda and taking Emma's file from her hand. "Sorry, she's spoken for." The tall blonde shrugged, understanding that these things are a messy situation.

He handed me the file. "Are you sure?"

"Ninety-nine percent. Just need to skim this."

He flashed a grin. "You haven't called the first choice in a long time. She's yours."

A wave of relief washed over me, then again when I skimmed the pages distilling Emma's life into a few sheets of paper. Nothing raised red flags, or sounded like more than I could handle. I could take her home right now and train her to be my submissive.

I wasn't sure whether I should run in and take her away so she could stop worrying, or begin teaching her proper submission immediately. Torn between wanting to make the most of a learning experience, or being sweet to a nervous girl, I watched her through the glass for a moment, pondering.

For the first time in my life, I was nervous about a girl. I knew that she wanted me to be her Master. I knew that I would be thrilled to have her as my submissive. All signs pointed to us being a good team, and it was only for a month.

Once the other Dominants had made their choices and everything was sorted, they began calling submissives names, escorting them into private meeting rooms to have a little chat before taking them home. Emma looked so tiny, sitting on the edge of the couch, holding her purse in front of her. She alternated between staring at the floor and glancing up at the mirrored glass.

I asked Miranda to call her for me. "Emma," her seductive voice announced over the speaker, "Please exit through the south door and walk down the hall."

She nodded, standing slowly, then did as she was told. I opened the door a crack to watch her walking down the hallway, looking around for wherever she was supposed to go.

"She's lovely, Darren," Miranda said softly. "A bit green, but I'm sure you'll be a wonderful trainer for her."

"Thanks," I said with a smile, then I followed Emma down the hallway silently.

When she got to the end, I spoke before she could turn around.

"Face your Master and kneel."

She spun, obviously delighted at the sound of my voice, obeying immediately.

*** HEARING MASTER'S VOICE ***

I tried to remember everything I'd ever read about staying calm while I sat in this lounge filled with pretty goth girls. I wasn't very goth, or glam, and was the only one who was wearing a plain black dress instead of a complicated leather and chain outfit.

Would Darren take a look at these other women and want someone else? Would he change his mind? Would he want someone who had more experience in bondage, so that he could train them at a more expert level? Or, and this was the question that worried me the most, would he not want to train me because I practically jumped him? Just because my self-control lapsed once doesn't mean that's who I am.

A dark thought filled my mind as I tried to stare at the carpet while taking deep breaths. Would he not want to keep me because I was too small for him, and he could only work his way halfway inside me? He said he wasn't as interested in the sex part, but the chemistry we had immediately was unbelievable. He had to have felt it too. The way he grabbed me, the way that dark, raw voice filled my ears. I had to force myself not to visibly quiver.

I'd never felt such a thrill. The way he pinned me, owned me. And that was only for a few minutes in a parking lot. I could feel myself blushing again just thinking about if someone had caught us. What would he do with me if I was living with him for a month?

Positive thoughts, I told myself, even though my entire body was still humming. I stared at the floor, attempting to be calm, knowing that my fate was being decided behind that glass.

Then a woman's smoky voice came over the speaker. "Emma, please exit through the south door and walk down the hall."

I automatically nodded and stood up. Was I going with

a woman? On my application I had marked that I was bi-
curious, but I hadn't even thought of a Mistress taking me
instead of a Master.

Walking down the hall, I looked around to see where I
was supposed to go. There were no doors open. I didn't want
to go poking around in this huge mansion. Should I just
wait?

"Face your Master and kneel."

That voice. I spun in a flash, meeting his eyes before
dropping to my knees awkwardly. Looking up at him, that
strong, sculpted face, those thick arms and huge chiseled
chest. His dark, warm eyes were smiling down at me even
when he tried to appear stern. He was far rougher than any
man who had ever caught my eye, but somehow I trusted
him.

He stepped toward me, placing a finger under my chin.
"Do you agree to be mine for a month?"

"Yes, Sir," I whispered.

"Stand."

I obeyed immediately. I was so relieved, excited,
anxious to get started, that I was trembling.

His arms circled me in a blink, pulling me into my chest.
"You're shaking like a leaf. Listen, we can just spend the
first few days figuring out everything you want to learn,
okay? Just because we started out… well, strangely intimate,
doesn't mean that's what I'm after."

"I am," I said, stretching up on my toes to kiss him.
His heat enveloped me, his big hands gripped my ass, and
our bodies pressed together quite indecently right in the
hallway of Master Jeremy's mansion. My lips parted and his
tongue entered my mouth tentatively, then possessing me
completely. I moaned, unable to control myself. I realized
the only thing I wanted in this world was for him to lie me
on the floor right here.

Darren shoved me away, holding my shoulders at arm's

length. "You naughty little brat," he said, trying to be stern, but his eyes were smiling.

"I'm sorry, Sir. I couldn't help it."

He shook his head, his tousled black hair swinging. "Do you need to get your stuff?"

"My suitcase is in the front hall."

"Let's go."

I giggled as we walked to his car, my eyes darting at the streaks on the front hood that marred the perfect finish.

"Don't worry, I'll have you scrub the car tomorrow. Naked."

I laughed, then cocked my head as I became less certain that he was joking. "I hope it's an indoor garage," I laughed.

"No. But the neighbors probably won't notice."

We got in and he began driving quickly with that confident air of someone who grew up around cars. Then he cleared his throat, shooting me a sideways glance.

"It's a little unusual that you signed up to be taken away as a submissive for thirty days when you don't know very much about the whole S&M lifestyle."

I shrugged. "I need a life change. I don't start my new job for six weeks, and I've always been curious about this stuff." I stared into space for a moment, trying to figure it out myself. "I guess I'm the sort of person who wants to jump all in when something interests me. I don't want to read a book about it, and think about it for months at a time. Just go."

He nodded, thinking. "I guess I could see that."

We drove in comfortable silence for a bit, farther outside of the city than I expected.

"I hope you're not expecting a huge mansion like Jeremy's," he said, that low, gruff voice making my insides flip. "It's just a normal house."

"I don't care."

"Oh the plus side, since you'll be the one cleaning it

will be less work for you."

"I'm going to be your maid?"

He chuckled. "No. You'll be my sub. My pet. A proper submissive must learn service. Every time you're on your knees scrubbing the floor, you'll be concentrating on doing a perfect job for your Master. It's to teach patience, and help ground you in your place."

As we turned a corner, his thick forearm and hand caught the glow of a streetlight. Looking over at him, I realized again that he was a really big man. I was going to be in his house, at his mercy. I was really going to be his little toy.

Any normal woman would have been nervous. Possibly even terrified. Instead, I felt myself becoming wet. My nipples began to feel sensitive, and I could feel my heart starting to pound.

*** MASTER'S HOUSE ***

We pulled into a long driveway at the far edge of the city, almost a quarter-mile away from the main road. There were two motorbikes parked in front, one of them a giant old Harley that gleamed as the car's headlights passed over it.

It was quite secluded. The house itself was much larger than he let on, likely at least five bedrooms, with huge front windows overlooking a lovely wild English garden.

We walked into the front hall, and I figured he would show me to his room right away. Instead, he opened a drawer in the large antique desk that was functioning as a hallway table. There were several small leather collars inside, and as he reached in, he gave me the strangest glance. I saw that several of them were black, but he selected a slim white one with a silver ring in the front.

The thought of him tying me up by my collar like a puppy sent a shiver through me. That would be a strange feeling of possession, I was pretty sure.

"Strip." His deep voice rang through the hallway.

"What?"

He smiled, a seductive, slightly crooked grin. "Submissives are to be naked in my home. You may wear an apron when cooking, you'll see them on a hook in the kitchen. But you'll be wearing nothing but this collar for a month."

I could feel him searching my eyes, making sure that I was okay with this. I'd always been fairly confident about my body, having spent so many years in ballet and modern dance. I knew that I was slim and toned. But was I what he was looking for?

I started to make a crack, then felt my lips lock as a need to submit washed over me. Nodding, I set down my things, slipped off my shoes, and unzipped my dress. Sliding it down, the fabric fell to my feet, and I looked up at him, completely naked. Then I knelt in front of him.

Everything felt strange. I was giving myself away. It was my choice, and I had a safe word, and I knew that I could call it off at any time, but it still felt real. Maybe this was part of the game. The role play.

His huge hand stroked my hair, and I felt myself stretching up slightly into his touch like a cat. "My sweet little girl," he murmured. "I promise to take excellent care of you."

He fastened the collar around my neck. The slight pressure on my throat made me sit up a bit straighter.

"You're a vision," he said softly.

I felt myself blushing. "Are we the only people here?"

"Yes."

"May I sleep in your bed?" The words flew out before I could stop them.

"No."

My bottom lip stuck out as I stared up at him. Then he bent down to grip it between his teeth. My tongue flicked over his thumb as I stared up at him. In a split second I was in his arms, being carried down a flight of stairs to a dark room. He flipped a switch with his elbow, and dim, amber lights revealed a classic black and red dungeon room.

Darren threw me on the black bedspread of the huge bed in the corner. I was naked, small and pale against the darkness, and loved the way his eyes wandered over me.

He pulled off his t-shirt, and I heard myself gasp. That body was unreal. He must have thought I was scared instead of impressed, as he leaned in to kiss me gently.

"I'll never hurt you in a bad way, I swear, little girl. I know I look like a big scary guy, but I promise you, if I even think you're going to say the word 'red' I'll stop."

I nodded, reaching out to stroke the muscles of his chest. "Please, I need you." I'd never heard myself beg before, and was surprised at how out of control I felt around him.

He stood back up to kick off his shoes and yank off his jeans. My mouth actually began watering as I saw his thick, juicy cock. I was determined to train my body to take him completely. There had to be a way. A shudder of pure lust went through me, and once again, he must have thought it was nerves. I had too much energy coursing through me, and it was making me shakey and strange.

"Shh, baby, it's okay," he murmured, laying beside me. "I know you're too small for me. We'll just work with what we've got."

Grabbing at his shoulders, I tried to pull him on top of me. He chuckled, then did what I wanted. "I'm supposed to be the one in control here, you hot little brat."

I couldn't answer, my lips took over as my hands wound into the back of his hair and my entire body began grinding up against him. I'd never been this hot for anyone before, and I felt like an animal. Out of control. Being run by lust and adrenaline.

How could I make him need this as much as I did? By serving him. By letting him control me. That way we could both get what we want.

"Get up on all fours," I ordered, and he was so surprised that he did it. I scooted down under him until his hips were above my head, gripping his massive cock in both hands.

Flickering my tongue around the tip, I loved the little sound of his soft groan. Licking quickly up and down the length, he shifted position, getting comfortable. Once he was nice and wet, I pulled him between my lips. Between my mouth and both hands, I had him almost completely covered. Swallowing as much as possible, I stroked his length, finding a slow pace he seemed to enjoy.

Then I stopped, staying completely motionless.

"Oh fuck," he breathed, realizing what I wanted. His hips began to carefully propel him until he was fucking my mouth. I couldn't stifle my moaning. This gorgeous, hot man was both under my control, and using me for his pleasure. The tension was building through my core and I felt my pussy becoming so wet I was likely dripping on the bedspread.

"Mmm," I moaned louder, opening my throat so he could glide deeper.

"Fucking your pretty little face is so wrong," he groaned. "Baby, are you gonna swallow?"

"Mmm hmm." I couldn't wait to drink him in, to please him. I was quivering, so aroused by his pleasure. Was this the service he was talking about? I could serve him all day, and all night. I began humming, letting the vibrations stimulate him even more. Stroking him faster with my hands, I tried to take him a little deeper.

I'd never had anyone let loose and fuck my mouth. It was the hottest thing I'd ever done. I felt all of my walls coming down around this guy, and every primal, reckless desire rushing to the surface. His pace increased and I felt his huge cock swelling between my lips.

"Emma…" he choked, then he was coming gloriously down my throat, his hot, slightly salty release filling my mouth as I swallowed as quickly as I could. He took a few more gentle strokes between my lips, then flipped us over, pulling me up so that I was laying on his chest.

Darren looked at me so dreamily that I felt my heart melting. Then his eyes narrowed. "Naughty little brat," he growled. "Taking advantage of your Master."

"I couldn't help it," I whispered. "I need you."

He kissed me hard, roughly, taking my breath away. Then he stared at me oddly. "I'm the one who will tell you what you need. Do you understand? You belong to me now. You do only what I tell you. Nothing more, nothing less. Your only thoughts will be how to obey me more precisely."

"Okay," I said, but my knees fell to the sides of his hips, as my open, wet pussy began grinding against his shaft as it began to stiffen.

He was a solid ten inches, and I'd only been able to take perhaps four inches or so before. I wondered how long it would be before I could take him all, or if that was even possible. But if I managed to practice several times a day, I was sure I could open for him.

I couldn't believe how wet I was, or how much I needed him. He was so powerful and strong that swaying his will to suit me gave me through that I couldn't even make sense of.

His kiss was electric, and I felt my cheeks flushing with desire as I wriggled on top of him. Reaching down, I spread my pussy lips over his shaft, moaning as I gently slid along his length.

Darren kissed me deeply, his hungry tongue invading my mouth, filling me just like I wanted to be filled below.

His hands cupped my breasts, feeling my hard nipples against his rough palms. Feeling how much he wanted me was absolutely delicious, and I slid my hands along his wide shoulders in pure adoration.

I felt a strange urge to submit to him, but a slightly more powerful urge to rebel against him. It seemed to fluster him, as if it's never happened before. Perhaps such a huge alpha male type wasn't accustomed to a tiny girl holding her own against him.

Sliding my hand down his heavily muscled chest, I pressed into his chiseled abs, lifting my hips so he could watch my pussy dancing over his cock.

A low, deep groan emanated from his chest, and I giggled at him, delighted to have him under my power. I'd never felt so drawn to anyone before, especially when I'd known them less than one day. But here I was, grabbing his mammoth shaft and guiding the head into my tight slit.

"Careful, baby," he murmured. "I know you're eager, but I can't let you hurt yourself."

I nudged the round, thick head inside me, then begin

lowering myself excruciatingly slowly. His eyes flashed back and forth between mine, and the place where we were joined.

"I love that you want to watch my pussy stretch around your cock, Sir."

He grabbed my ass with both hands, holding me steady. "I know that my good little girl wants it all, but take your time, sweetheart."

I nodded, unable to silence the soft moans that escaped me as I felt his thick head sinking inside me. It was incredibly tight, but I was so wet, so eager, that I felt him slide inside me a bit. Wriggling my hips slowly, I worked him a tiny bit deeper.

"You feel so amazing inside me," I gasped.

"You're so tight, baby. So tiny. Be careful."

I bent down to kiss his nose, then whispered, "I like that you take care of your property."

He chuckled, as I lowered another thick inch of his long shaft inside me. Rocking slowly, steadily up and down, he was soon a bit deeper than before.

"Oh fuck," I moaned, "I've never been so full."

His hands gripped me tighter, giving my ass a little shake. "You will watch your language, baby."

I laughed, but he gave my ass a tiny smack. "I'm serious. No pet of mine will have a foul mouth."

Placing my hands on his chest, I swiveled my hips, working him deeper. "I'm sorry, Sir. I was just so excited to have your beautiful cock so deep in my tight little cunt."

His eyes were absolutely burning with desire and frustration. I knew that his attention was split between wanting to train me and wanting to enjoy me, and it felt deliciously naughty to be teasing him like this.

Leaning back slightly, I gave him a fabulous view of every stroke, bucking up then lowering myself down as much as possible until I could not stretch any further. I was able to take a bit more than half of his length now, and it was a gloriously tight fit. Almost more stimulation and I could mentally process. Moving his hands to my hips, he began helping me, as we found a slow, deep rhythm.

"I want to watch you rub your clit while you ride my cock," he said in that hoarse, dark voice that drove me wild.

It was the first order that I didn't want to obey. I was still learning how to be open with my body, and comfortable being naked in front of men, but to touch myself in front of him... I didn't know if I could do it.

He saw my hesitation, and his lips quirked up in a crooked grin. "Your Master gave you a command, sweet girl. Obey."

His dark tone rumbled through me, and my hand lifted from his chest, settling between my legs as I touched my clit with two fingers. I began to circle gently, and within moments was already on the edge.

The way he tuned his attention on me completely was a first for me. He genuinely seemed more concerned with my pleasure than his.

Gripping my waist tighter, his hips rolled up into me, driving his thickness a few millimeters deeper. I've never been taken like this before, and it truly felt like he was claiming me, owning me.

"Does my sweet little baby want to be my good girl?"

"Yes,"

"Does my sexy girl want to come while riding her Master's cock?"

My breath seized in my throat as his thrusts became a tiny bit more intense. My insides were twitching, my thighs were clenching, and I was right on the very edge.

"That's my good girl," he said, his voice even deeper, gravelly. "I can feel that your sweet little pussy wants to obey me."

I heard a strange noise it sounded like a strangled

squeal, then the most intense orgasm of my life washed over me like a tidal wave, as I shook uncontrollably.

"Oh fuck… Emma…" He groaned, his fingers digging into me as he buried himself inside me. I could feel him throbbing, then he was spurting deep in my pussy, filling me with his hot cum.

"Yes, oh yes Master," I squealed, losing myself completely.

Collapsing on top of him, we kissed savagely for several minutes before we eventually stopped, staring at each other in surprise.

*** DAMMIT, EMMA ***

"Dammit, Emma," he laughed, laying flat on his back beside me. His fingers entwined with mine, and we held hands as our breathing settled. Then he propped himself up on his elbow, turning to me. "You know that you're going to have to obey me, right?"

I nodded, trying not to be mouthy, even as I felt words welling up in my mouth.

"You're going to have to learn my rules, submit to me, and become my little pet."

I curled up slightly, hopefully looking small and pale against the black bed, grinning. "You like that you're so huge and I'm so tiny, don't you?"

His lips pressed together, trying not to laugh. "Yes." He reached out to run his fingertips around the curve of my breast. "You're so perfect. A little doll."

"I'm going to stretch for you," I said matter of factly. He seemed a bit shocked that I was so determined. "Your massive cock is going to stretch me open until I can take you all."

Rolling on top of him again, I spread my legs, rubbing my cum soaked pussy lips against his quickly thickening shaft. "Would you like that? Do you want to shape my body for you? Would that make it feel even more like you owned me?"

In a flash I was flipped onto my back. I heard a rattle of chains, and looked up to see him pulling leather cuffs from a hidden shelf just behind the headboard. He quickly fastened them on me so that my wrists were held straight over my head. At first I wondered why my arms weren't spread wide, but then I realized that the chains were long enough that he could flip me over this way.

He placed his hand in the center of my chest in a strangely calming gesture. "You're captured. You're mine.

How does that make you feel?"

"Fuck me. Now. Please."

Darren's chuckle was absolutely adorable. "So, you'd say that being tied down fills you with desire?"

"I'm not kidding. Please, get your cock into me."

He ignored me. "Remember your safe words?"

"Green, yellow, red."

"When do you call yellow?"

"When you're not fucking me, and I need it."

"Come on. Be serious for a minute."

I rolled my eyes. "This is the one part I did study. Yellow is for when I really need a break, or water, or any of the ties or equipment needs adjusting, or I'm getting near my limit."

"And red?"

"Is for when I need you to stop completely."

"Yes. And you have my absolute word that if you ever say red, I will stop, untie you, care for you completely." His thumb stroked my cheek gently. "I'll always be watching you carefully, so I don't think we'd ever get to that point. But if you think you're near your limit, be sure to say red a moment before you need to, never after. Okay?"

"Yellow."

"What's wrong?" He wasn't sure if he should actually be concerned, but he checked the tightness of my cuffs automatically.

"My pussy is empty and it's driving me crazy."

Darren paused, looking at me strangely. I was pretty sure he had no idea what to do with me. Maybe all the girls he's ever been with were obedient little pets from the very first moment. But I couldn't focus, could barely breathe. Having him beside me, over me, that huge wall of muscle in my face as he leaned in to check the cuffs... I couldn't stay still.

Lunging up, I managed to get my lips within a few

inches of his, and he fell into my kiss, guiding me back down so that he was nearly on top of me. Our lips moved as one, and I could feel that he was aroused by the way he had me captured. I could use this.

"You have a tiny girl in your evil playroom. If you don't play with her, what's the point of this room?" I giggled sweetly.

"You're too pretty to be this naughty," he said.

"Thank you. But I'm not naughty. I've never been like this before. My body needs you – I can't help it."

"You need discipline. Don't worry, baby. You'll learn."

"I need you inside me. Please." Perhaps it was my begging tone, or my wide eyes, but he looked less determined.

"Good little submissives know their place."

"My place is under you while you fill me." I strained at the cuffs, needing to get to him. "If you want to shut me up, ram your cock into my mouth," I whined.

I've never behaved like this in my life, it was like I was being overcome by a spoiled, bratty slut.

I was flipped over, and his hand lightly spanked my ass a few times. Digging my knees into the bed, I pressed up, hoisting my backside into the air while spreading my legs wide. "You can't leave me like this, still dripping with your cum, needing more," I whispered, shaking my ass in front of his face.

Instead of another smack, I felt his finger circle my wet inner lips. Rocking back against him very slightly, his finger slipped inside.

"Thank you, Sir," I said softly, and I was rewarded with another finger. Looking back over my shoulder, his face was tense. Perhaps he was having an internal war with his libido and his urge to be an appropriate dominant.

"You promised to take care of me," I whispered. "Thank you for giving me what I need, Sir." Moving against his hand, he was now thrusting deep into my greedy pussy.

"Emma, you're such a bad girl," he growled, and there was no way he didn't see the shudder that ran through me.

"Yes, but I'm your bad girl," I giggled. Then I moaned, as he plunged a bit deeper. "Let me have my hands so I can stroke your cock," I begged.

"No." Glancing back again, he was grinning.

I spread my legs wider. "Don't you want to fuck your little submissive? Show me who's boss? Control me?"

His fingers lowered to graze my clit, sending sparks straight through me. "I should control you by leaving you here alone for an hour to think about how naughty you are."

"But I could be serving you, and your huge cock." I turned to watch his eyes while I said, "You could practice stretching me open for you." He liked that, I could see it. My body being molded to his aroused him.

"The more you open me, the more you show me I'm yours, and the more obedient I'll be," I said gently, clasping my hands as my hips pressed back into his fingers.

He knew exactly how to work my clit, and I felt the waves gathering deep in my core already.

"Oh, Sir… You're going to make me come while I'm empty. Wouldn't you like to feel my pussy clenching around you?"

Sneaking a peek, I saw him stroking his enormous dick in one hand while he fingered me. Placing his thick head between my pussy lips, I sighed with relief as he pressed inside a little.

"Thank you, Sir," I breathed, gently pressing back.

Darren knelt behind me, pulling my hips up so that I could do the rocking, opening myself at my own pace. He likely thought I'd be gentle, since he seemed very concerned about hurting me. Instead, I thrust back quickly and deeply several times, wedging at least half of his thickness inside me.

"Careful, baby," he said, but he must have loved the feeling.

"I can't help it." Impaling myself over and over, I worked him steadily deeper while his fingers swirled over my swollen clit.

Being tied like this was driving me wild, and I felt like I was completely out of control. I was high as a kite on adrenaline, and couldn't stop the orgasm about to hit me hard.

"I... Yes... Oh fuck, Darren," I wailed, as my climax slammed through me. It was too much pleasure, rippling through me with an intensity I'd never experienced before, and I was already addicted. My pussy walls were clutching him tightly, massaging him as he took over, starting to fuck me.

My wrists were pulling at the chains, not to try to escape, but because every part of me was flailing.

"That's my good girl," he said, stroking my back. "Coming all over your Master's cock." His dark voice actually prolonged the spasms, as the release continued to flow through me.

"I want to serve you," I breathed, "I do."

Coming back to earth, the pressure of him inside me was a lot to process. Trying to relax, I felt him slide a bit deeper. "Are you all the way inside me?"

He chuckled. "Almost two thirds, baby. I'm impressed." Both of his hands were around my waist now as I stayed still, letting him fuck me slowly. I'd never felt anything so intoxicating in my life. The friction was incredible as his shaft rubbed snugly against my delicate walls with every stroke.

"You feel so perfect," he groaned.

"I need to please you," I whimpered, not even realizing what I was saying. "I want you to need me as much as I need you."

His cock throbbed inside me even more. "I do need you, gorgeous. You feel so good…"

"Harder," I begged. "Please, Sir, fill me again."

I looked back to see his glazed eyes as he watched his monster cock sinking into my little pink twat. He looked like he was right on the edge, as he picked up speed very slightly.

"You're stretching me open," I moaned. "I couldn't believe I fit a few inches of you, but this… Oh, Sir, please… more…" I heard myself wailing. "Fuck me harder. Make me take it."

His deep grunt as he began pounding harder filled me with a satisfaction I couldn't understand. Was this submission? Putting the Master first, playing his game? The feelings washing through me were strange and more intense than I could ever have anticipated.

"Yes," I moaned, "Sir… You're stretching me…"

Darren growled as he rammed me a few more strokes, and I somehow felt him shift a bit deeper as he came hard, filling me with thick bursts of his hot juice.

"Mmm more…" I murmured, wriggling under him as he finally slowed his pace.

He became still, and I looked back as he pulled out, watching his cum drip down my legs. "I love that I'm your little slut now," I whispered, and he looked shocked as he met my eyes.

Uncuffing me quickly, he sat up with his back against the headboard, sitting me in his lap. "You're not my slut," he said carefully. "You're my submissive. You're my toy, my pet, but with the highest respect. We give ourselves to each other. Do you understand?"

I nodded, giggling. "Yes. But feeling slutty for you is incredibly hot."

He chuckled, and I felt a rumble in the shoulder that was pressed into his chest. "Okay, that's fine. I don't want you to think for one second that I really think of you that way."

Tipping my chin up with his finger, he looked into my eyes with an expression I'd never seen before. "I think you're incredibly brave," he said softly. "Throwing yourself into a world you don't know much about. You really should have studied a lot more before you signed up, but I'm delighted that you're here now."

I kissed him gently, wrapping my arms around his neck. He melted against me, his hands stroking my back, then he pulled away. "You're touching your Master without permission again," he said, trying to seem stern.

"And you can punish me tomorrow." I snuggled my head against his shoulder. "I'll try to learn some of this stuff properly."

"Good girl." He met my eyes again. "I've been calling you little girl, baby, without even thinking. You're just so tiny and beautiful that it seems natural. Is that okay with you?"

I nodded, feeling my cheeks flush. "I've never liked it before, but it's different with you." I paused. "A lot of things are different with you."

Darren nodded. "It's a weird situation. We'll talk everything out, and we'll be fine. Right?"

"Right."

"Right, what?"

I stared at him blankly, then giggled. "Right, Sir."

"That's better." He was almost rocking me in his lap, and I felt more satiated, more satisfied than I'd ever felt in my life. "Now that we've hopefully gotten that out of our systems,, tomorrow we'll begin your training properly."

We got up slowly, and I loved the way he kept an arm around me, as if I were some fragile little dove he needed to care for. We went back upstairs, and he carried my suitcase to a small purple and white bedroom. "Your washroom is across the hall. Holler if you need anything."

Throwing my purse on the bed, I spun to wrap my arms

Lexie Renard

around his neck, surprising him with a deep, sexy kiss. "All I need is you," I whispered. "Stay with me tonight."

"No, baby. We need a little space."

"Okay," I pouted, adoring the way his gaze studied my bottom lip. "But if you get lonely, you know where I am."

He kissed me again, that strange heat rising between us. But he stopped it too soon. "Sweet dreams, little girl."

Shutting the door behind him, he left me alone. It had always pissed me off when people called me little, or a girl instead of a woman. But Darren... when he said it, a thrill flashed through me. I wanted to be his little girl so badly.

There must be a way for me to learn his ways, and be his pet properly. Tomorrow I would try much harder to learn and follow the rules. Then I giggled to myself. Until I got distracted by that incredible body and deep eyes. Then I'd be throwing myself at him again, especially now that I knew how to push some of his buttons.

***

Polishing Emma
(BDSM Training School Book #5)

*** THE BDSM ACADEMY ***

The BDSM Academy is rarely spoken of beyond a whisper. But if you beg the owners, organizers, and Dominants of the most respected dungeons, they may pass your name along for consideration.

Seven of the most respected Dominants and Dominatrixes in the city banded together to create an informal program where submissives could learn as much as they wanted about the BDSM world in a safe environment.

They were tired of seeing newcomers so desperate for the experience that they allowed less than reputable "Masters" and "Mistresses" to pick them up. With no experience, guidance, or mentorship, it was far too easy for abusive and manipulative people to take advantage of them.

To sign up for the BDSM Academy, applicants must commit to a thirty-day, twenty-four-seven submissive lifestyle, giving themselves completely to the whims of their Master or Mistress. This will ensure that they are extremely serious, and allow them to completely fall into the submissive headspace, learn about the lifestyle, and discover what they really wanted for themselves.

One can only determine what one truly needs from a Dominant if one has been dominated.

*** THE KITCHEN ***

I should be angry. I should be putting her over my knee and giving her the spanking of a lifetime. But instead, I gripped the back of her hair, moaning while she opened her throat, taking me deeper.

Her sweet, bright eyes looked up at me from where she knelt on the floor, serving me. Her hands were clasped behind her back so that I was able to pull her closer. Her face was slightly flushed, her pupils wide. It was a thrill that she was as aroused as I was. I've never met a girl who adored giving head as much as Emma.

She pressed her lips tighter against my shaft, sucking deeply as I took long, slow thrusts into her throat. Her eyes were smiling, and she looked positively delighted.

Five minutes ago I had ordered her to scrub the kitchen floor, telling her where the bucket and brush were, expecting to come back to see her on her hands and knees. Instead, when I returned she was just on her knees, hands behind her back, thrusting those luscious tits out while she looked up at me.

"Your master gave you an order."

Emma opened her mouth slightly, licking her lips. "But I know what Master really needs," she said.

She lunged for me, her nimble fingers pulling my pants down and pulling my half-hard shaft into her mouth before I could even blink. Her soft little palms ran along my skin, getting me completely stiff for her in seconds.

I wasn't sure which was hotter – that she threw herself at me constantly, giving herself as my adorable sex pet, or the way she grinned up at me, knowing that she was being a disgraceful naughty brat.

She scooted closer on her knees, positioning herself under me then clasped her wrists at the back, offering me her mouth completely. She began fluttering her tongue underneath my shaft, sucking harder and bobbing her head to help me take faster strokes.

Both my knees and my resolve became weak. I couldn't help it. As much as I was determined to be her dominant, her master, I was also a hot-blooded man looking down at her creamy breasts, and sweet lips wrapped around my dick.

My hand wound into the back of her soft blonde hair before I even knew what was happening. She clung to me, her hot, wet mouth sucking hard as she rocked her head forward. She alternated between butterfly soft caresses and a long hard sucks. Her dedication to my pleasure was admirable, even though she was being brazenly disobedient.

I couldn't stop. It was like an out of body experience. Leaning into her tender mouth, I begin burrowing deeper, taking smooth, deep strokes as her shimmering eyes smiled up at me. The rougher I became, the more delighted she seemed.

I desperately needed to throw her backward and bury myself inside her, but then her tongue began fluttering harder against my sensitive head, and she tilted her head back to take me deeper down her throat. Gripping her tightly with both hands, I began fucking her pretty little face harder until she moaned with delight.

"You're such a bad girl," I heard myself growl, and her eyes absolutely blazed.

She released her hands from her back, massaging the very base of my shaft while she caressed my balls. Gripping her harder, my hips plunged my cock down her throat several more times before I exploded into her sexy mouth.

Her choked little moan was followed by huge swallows, taking me deep as she devoured every drop and licked me clean. Stepping back, I felt dazed.

"Baby, was that too rough?"

She shook her head, grinning, then wiping her mouth dramatically with the back of her hand. "I love it when you use me as your little sex toy," she whispered, delicately licking her lips again.

"Emma, that was fabulous–"

"Thank you, Sir," she said quickly, looking proud of herself.

"But you still need to scrub the floor. It's a basic chore, and you haven't done a single thing all day." Her face was starting to scrunch up into a glare, and I grabbed her by the chin. "Baby, please. Just one chore. Take that first step for me."

She pouted, and the urge to put her over my knee was overwhelming, but it made us both so hot it wasn't really going to help.

"Now," I growled, trying to look stern.

"Yes, Sir," she sighed, crawling over to the bucket.

I went to my office to force myself to check my email. Anything to distract me from knowing that hot little brat was just down the hall. I had no idea how I was going to find a way to control myself. But I had to. I had to educate her. She had signed up to learn a month's worth of information, and I wasn't a very good teacher if I couldn't keep it in my pants for more than two minutes around her.

I couldn't tell if it was her breathtaking scent, the way she wanted me so savagely, or what, but I found myself unsteady with a woman for the first time ever.

I'd never felt this sort of pull before. Like I was already addicted to her.

Waiting twenty minutes, I returned to the kitchen to see the floor sparkling clean, with Emma kneeling in the corner. There was no way she had done it by hand as I had instructed, and it would have been easy for her to find the mop in the closet practically behind her.

But the job was done, so at least that was a small victory.

*** THE COUNTER ***

If he wasn't watching me on my hands and knees, there was no way I was going to do such an annoying task. The floor got washed, so he should be happy with that. I didn't really intend to disobey him this time, it's just that I really hate housework.

I could tell by the look in his eyes though, Darren wasn't buying it. But he also wasn't sure what to do. I held my head up high, knowing that he loved the way I was naked except for my little white leather collar.

I looked up at him through my eyelashes. "How else may I serve you, Sir?"

My eyes flickered to the bulge forming in his jeans, and I licked my lips at him. I have never felt this wildly sexual before, and adored the way his presence made me absolutely crazy with lust.

He looked around the room carefully. "You didn't wipe the counters."

Dammit. I cringed. "I'm sorry, Sir. Your cock was so delicious earlier that I forgot."

"Up."

He snapped his fingers and I stood up, taking a few steps forward to stand right in front of him. I knew he liked how tiny I was, and I actually felt myself shrinking down a bit more as I looked up at him.

"You know that I have to punish you, right? It's not my choice. You chose this dynamic, and now you're going to have to face the consequences."

His low voice was becoming thicker, rougher, and I could tell he was right on the edge of deciding what to do with me.

"Would you like me on my knees again for you?" I asked sweetly.

"I'm serious, Emma. This time I'm afraid it has to be

done.".

Taking me by the shoulders, he turned me so that I was facing the kitchen counter. "Put your hands on the edge, and spread your legs."

I got into position, tossing my short blond hair as I looked back over my shoulder at him. I knew he loved to admire my ass, so I squirmed slightly as I thrust it up toward him. "Like this?" I asked innocently.

His huge hands settled around my waist, pulling my hips farther back. "This is a house of discipline, little one. Obeying the rules is simple. You just have to choose to be a good pet."

The heat of his hands skimming across my skin was driving me wild, and I could feel my pulse beginning to race already.

It was strange being completely naked while he was fully clothed, but it aroused me even more. The palm of his hand slid along the curve of my ass, caressing me gently, but I knew what was coming. It was so hard not to squirm, but I tried to be still for him.

His hand quickly came down with a smack, the sting ringing through my ass and sending an electric zap of pain through my body. But it felt so fucking good.

Then his hand smacked the other side, tempting me to cry out but I tried to stay silent. I felt my pussy tingling with desire and actually worried that I might drip on the freshly washed floor. My legs instinctively began to slide together, but he smacked me again, then pressed my feet a bit farther apart with his foot.

"Are you trying to hide your pretty little pussy from me?"

I didn't know how to answer him.

His hand came down hard across my ass cheek again, sending heat shivering straight through me until I whimpered softly.

"For as long as you are in my house, this is my sweet little twat. Do you understand?" He cupped it gently in his hand, running his fingers through my folds.

"Yes, Sir," I whispered, my thighs beginning to tremble.

I may have heard a low growl coming from his throat. I couldn't believe that he was spanking me while I stood up like this. I felt so exposed, so crazily vulnerable that it was cranking my adrenaline through the roof. He slapped my ass sharply again and this time I squealed.

His palm instantly rubbed the spot gently, taking the sting out. Glancing back at him again, I saw him staring between my legs, and my breathing began to hitch. I wanted him. I needed him. Needed him to fuck me until I couldn't see.

He smacked the opposite side, and I couldn't stop the long, low moan from ringing through the room. My hips raised up as if I were trying to will him to touch me again.

"Are you wet for your Master?" he asked, his voice even darker.

"I think so, Sir, but you should probably check."

His hand slid between my legs, prying my wet lips open to slide a thick finger inside me.

"Yes, please," I whined, my hips moving of their own accord. His other hand tightened around my hip, pulling me back against him, and I gasped, almost off-balance.

"I won't let you fall, baby girl."

I turned back to look him in the eye. "I know. I trust you."

That seemed to do something to him, as he wrapped both hands around my waist, spinning me so that I was in his arms, kissing me hungrily. My arms circled his neck as I clung to him. I immediately pressed against his arousal, unable to stop myself.

"Please, Sir, spank me on the inside," I whimpered. "I need you so bad it hurts."

I pressed my face against the wall of muscle that was his chest, feeling his hands grabbing me tighter. Dropping my hands, I quickly unfastened his jeans, pushing them down until they fell to the floor. Then I ripped off his tight black T-shirt, unable to stop myself from staring at the unbelievable body of my new Master.

He helped me by pulling it over his head, then he gripped me tightly, "If this is what you want, you're going to have to take whatever I give you."

I looked up at him, nodding quickly. "Anything you want. I'm here to serve you, Sir."

Throwing my arms around his neck, I stretched up and kissed him. His mouth moved with mine perfectly, the heat rising between us.

I squealed against his lips as he grabbed me hard, gripping my ass as he lifted me and set me on the kitchen counter. Then I squealed again from the chill of the marble, which made him chuckle.

Opening my lips, I moaned softly as his tongue claimed my mouth. His fingers were still gripping my ass, pulling me right to the edge so that I was holding onto him tightly. His obscenely hard shaft was so thick it was practically pulsing as it slid along my upper thigh, toward its target.

"Do you think you can take more than two-thirds of it today?" he asked.

"I want to. I really do." I whispered, spreading my legs wide as I wrapped them around his hips.

He pushed the swollen head of his cock against my dripping pussy lips, and I thought I could feel the pre-cum mixing with my juices. Everything about him was so erotic it was too much to take.

"Please, Sir, fuck your little girl. Make me your toy."

His hips pushed forward, sliding an inch of his thickness inside my tight little cunt. I was positive that he secretly loved that he was far too big for me.

"Yes," I moaned, "Stretch me open. Make me yours."

I looked up to see his eyes absolutely burning with desire. Nobody has ever looked at me like that before, and it filled me with something I couldn't begin to describe. Easing another inch inside me, we began slowly writhing against each other.

"So precious, my little one," he murmured, kissing down my throat and arching me back so he could wrap his lip around my nipple.

Rocking my hips against him, I accepted another few inches of his ten inch shaft. Looking down, I measured as he pulled almost all the way out of me. He was at least halfway inside, and it was getting a little easier to take every time.

"Are you proud of me, Sir? Look how hard I'm trying to take your entire cock. Does that make me a good girl?"

He looked down, watching his shaft penetrate me in long slow strokes. He pushed a tiny bit deeper, experimenting to see how open I could be.

"Yes," I moaned. But I looked up to meet his eyes. "Stretch my pussy open for your gorgeous cock, Master."

I knew he loved it when I said that, and I knew that calling him by that name was like flipping a switch. He stopped being gentle, gripping me harder as he started to really fuck me. I couldn't stop the little cries of pleasure falling from my lips, and his deep low groan thrilled me to the core.

He drove his hips against me, working to press deeper, and the strange pressure of being filled too tightly was intoxicating. Then he slowed his furious pace for a moment, leaning me back away from him.

"Rub your clit for me. I want to watch you."

He knew how difficult that was for me. Touching myself is a private thing, but I wanted to please him.

He seemed even more aroused by my hesitation. "Do as you're told, little one. Take three fingers, and put them in your mouth. Now."

Looking up at him with wide eyes, I obeyed.

"Get your fingers nice and wet."

I nodded, sucking and licking my fingers, loving the fire in his eyes.

"Now lower your hand and press your fingers against your clit."

I did it very slowly, letting my hand tremble so he could see how shy I was. I wasn't even sure why I enjoyed playing this role for him. Moving my fingers in tiny, tentative circles, I could feel the waves gathering deep within immediately.

"Does that feel good, baby?"

"Yes, Sir."

"I need you to be right on the edge. I need you to tell me when you're close."

I nodded, swirling my fingers a little faster while he thrust into me at a steady pace.

I was so eager to obey every order when we were doing something sexual. The way he plunged inside me, deeper and deeper, I wanted so badly to take him completely and drive him insane.

"Does my sexy man want to watch me come? Do you like seeing my tiny little fingers dancing across my clit?" I leaned back so that he could get an even better view of his enormous cock filling me while my fingers obeyed his request.

"I'll always love watching you," he groaned, gripping the back of my head to tilt my lips up to his.

Then he yanked me a little closer, pushing carefully as he tried to burrow deeper. "So wet for me, baby girl. So sweet to give yourself to your new Master."

I nodded, falling completely under his spell. "I'm getting closer, Sir. Do you want me to come for you?"

He looked down to watch my quick fingers and the way my little pink lips were being pulled open with every stroke.

His lips kissed my throat, then gripped me firmly, almost a bite. "Yes. Come for me now."

The electric sparks dancing through my core started to wash over me, and I looked up at him with wide eyes as I begin to quiver against him. My eyes began to close as my climax started, but he quickly ordered, "Look at me. Watch my eyes when you come."

I whined in frustration at the weird intimacy, then fell into it completely, letting everything fall away as I obeyed him. Every muscle began to twitch as I was flooded with the force of the orgasm rushing through me. I heard a few strangled cries that sounded like a wild animal, and saw his luscious mouth quirk up in a strange smile.

"I love it when you come on my cock," he groaned, gripping my ass with both hands and beginning to pump into me even harder. I felt my body stretching for him, as my pussy convulsed and relaxed, gushing even more as I came.

"Oh fuck, baby," he groaned. He glanced down then looked at me, impressed. "You're taking at least seven inches, baby. I'm so fucking proud of you."

My fingers didn't stop rubbing my clit hard, and I felt the waves forming again already.

"Come inside me," I cried with more force than I expected.

He pulled his juicy cock all the way out of me, leaving me empty and twitching.

"I'm sorry, Sir," I muttered quickly. "I didn't mean to. I meant to say please. Please come inside me. I just want to make you happy."

He filled me again slowly, caressing me deep within as he slid his thickness back into my tight wet tunnel. He felt so good it was almost too much. Increasing his rhythm gradually, he thrust over and over, watching my eyes as I began to twitch and tingle again.

"Come again for me, my sweet little girl."

"Yes… Sir…" Then I was screaming, falling, digging my left hand into the back of his shoulder blades as I gripped him tight while he fucked me hard and deep.

His eyes were burning with lust as he throbbed inside me, then I felt him tense up before he released, his hot load filling me up while I squealed in ecstasy. He finally slowed his pace, taking a few more long gentle thrusts, then pulling out completely.

"Baby, you almost took it all."

He held me against his chest, obviously proud of me. It was a strange feeling. I'd never been with a man who obviously cared this much, and wanted to see me succeed at something.

I couldn't help but wonder what he would do if I actually started obeying him and giving into his bizarre rules and rituals. If my natural urge to rebel was keeping me from pleasing this gorgeous man, that was something that I would have to think about carefully.

*** ROPE LESSON ***

Although I always preferred to be naked in the playroom, even if I wasn't anticipating sex, today I wore a pair of black boxers. The thin fabric wasn't much of a defense, but it was symbolic.

Emma seemed eager to pay attention, kneeling naked on the huge bed in front of me while I explained I was going to tie her up in rope, to gauge her reactions and comfort.

I tried to focus on wrapping the soft rope around her wrists, but her writhing, naked body was tempting me beyond belief. She was messing with my focus. I had intended to test how comfortable she was with bondage, so I knew where I was starting. But it was obvious she was just dying for me to take her.

I've never had a woman who seemed to want me this much, who seemed to be going absolutely crazy for me.

Here I was thinking that I would teach her patience and control, yet the one who seemed to need it most in this case was certainly the dominant.

I tried to clear my head with a few deep breaths, finishing her wrist tie, then placing her on her front. I had intended to tie her ankles, fastening them up behind her bum so she was completely immobilized, but she instantly pulled herself up on her knees, spreading them wide and shaking her hot little peach of an ass at me.

"Please, Sir," she moaned. "Don't you want me?"

"Of course I do, baby. But I want you when you're obedient, and know your place."

She giggled. "My place is under you with my legs spread, learning how to take your giant biker cock."

Oh fuck, that saucy mouth. I was immediately hard as stone. Throwing her over my knee, her giggling stopped when I smacked her ass hard. Her little gasp of shock was followed by complete silence.

I'd studied anatomy, and talked with other dominants about the first strike. There was a perfect spot on the bottom of the cheek, slightly to the outside, where you could get maximum volume without as much pain. It was the element of surprise needed sometimes.

Having never dealt with a bratty submissive before, I felt that I needed to start controlling the situation before she developed any more bad habits. No matter what happened between us, a submissive that had been trained by me should go out into the world having learned a certain amount of discipline. Any less would reflect badly on me, and my training skills.

Although she became silent, I could feel the reaction in her body. She was unbelievably turned on. I smacked the other side, letting the sound ring through the room before asking, "Do I need to continue, or will you behave now?"

Her hips began writhing on my lap. "I… I don't know."

Smacking her twice more on each side, the feeling of my palm against her bare skin was driving us both crazy. She was so tiny that hitting her at all, even carefully and not very hard, seemed wrong. But she was squirming, her entire body begging for more.

"I'm sorry I've been naughty, Sir," she said softly. "I'll try harder."

Her words certainly didn't match her actions, as she wiggled her hot little mound against my cock firmly through my shorts.

"Emma, stop moving."

"I can't."

I smacked her again, a little harder, while watching her shoulder blades. She didn't even flinch. Instead, a little shiver ran through her, and she spread her thighs a tiny bit as if trying to work my cock between her legs. Her hips swiveled until my thick head was wedged against her clit as she humped me shamelessly right through my shorts.

She was practically feral, the way she was rubbing against me wildly.

"Emma, be still."

"Oh fuck, Sir, spank me a little more, please."

"Emma, you were disobeying a direct order."

"But isn't the most important order to please you?"

"Emma, look at me."

She looked up with a naughty grin, biting her lower lip. Her perfect tiny, curvy figure with those doll eyes and fall lips made her look like the ultimate sex kitten. Her hands were still bound with rope, white, to match her little collar.

"Baby, this time I'm going to actually have to discipline you. For real."

She draped herself over my lap more carefully, blatantly rubbing the top of her mound against the quickly growing bulge in my shorts.

I began slowly caressing her hot tight ass, while she moaned, still squirming. Then I brought my hand against her cheek with a sharp snap, this time stroking her with enough force that she squealed a slightly different way.

"Hey, what the hell?" she whined.

I gave her another smack, not being nearly as rough as I had been with previous submissives. But she wasn't used to a bit of actual pain. I held still for a moment, then gave her one more sharp crack against the underside of her sexy butt.

Something shifted inside her, and she seemed to relax into the sensation. Her squirming hips slowed down, becoming more sultry. I could feel my shorts becoming wet from her sweet pussy juice leaking onto me. Her hot little cheeks were now flushed pink.

"Would you like more spankings, getting harder every time? Or would you like to be my good girl now?"

"I'm yours," she whispered breathlessly.

She rolled onto her back, and I grabbed her so she wouldn't fall. Pulling her against me as she laid in my lap, she looked up at me with the strangest expression. "I'm trying. Really I am. But it's hard for me."

"I know baby."

I cradled her in my arms, then without even realizing I was doing it, my hand was gliding up her inner thigh, teasing open her soft wet folds, and tracing her inner pussy lips with the tip of my finger.

I needed to sink myself inside her softness immediately. More than I needed air. More than I've ever needed anything before. But that wasn't going to teach her a lesson.

"Rope bondage, Emma," I said softly. "Have you ever been tied up with rope?"

"No, sir."

Swinging her onto the bed, I said, "On all fours with your hands stretched up to the headboard."

She obeyed beautifully, her sweet little body stretched out for me as she crawled into position. Grabbing some more soft jute, I fastened her wrists to a ring in the headboard leaving her a foot of slack.

Then I tied each leg, wrapping the rope so that her calf was pressed up against her thigh as she balanced on her knees with her heels just under her bum. When I finished, her weight was on her elbows and knees, her ass thrust up in the air leaving me staring directly into her luscious open pussy.

"How do you feel, baby?"

"This is… It's a little scary. Sir," she added quickly.

I stroked her back gently. You know your safe words, right? Or just tell me if you've had enough."

"Yes. I'm okay. I'm just… It's a little overwhelming."

I brought my finger to her soft little lips again, swirling gently, barely dipping inside. "You aren't yourself right now, Emma. You're my submissive. It's like an alternate universe, where your entire existence is simply being mine. Some people say that it's refreshing to step outside of themselves."

I slowly slid my finger inside her as she moaned, her hips beginning to wiggle.

"Do you like it soft or hard?" I suddenly asked.

Emma looked back over her shoulder at me. "I like everything you do to me," she said. "Absolutely everything." She paused, then whispered almost under her breath, "Especially hard."

Pulling my finger out, I let her squirm for a moment before slipping it back inside her. Her soft little moan was adorable, and she began rocking back against my hand, fucking herself without even thinking.

"Please," she gasped, "Fill me up with that gigantic cock."

I grabbed her a bit roughly, spreading her legs wide. "Let's make sure you're wet enough to take me like this."

She stiffened. "What do you mean?"

"I want to taste your sweet little pussy."

"Then let me roll over onto my back."

"No, baby. Stay still."

She made a strange little noise as I lowered my tongue to her swollen wet pussy lips. She twitched away from me for a second, then begin to relax.

"What's wrong, baby?"

"It just seems… Weird like this."

"Relax. Just let your Master enjoy your sweet juices."

Running my tongue around her clit several times, I began licking her entire slit hard. She finally began to relax, realizing that there was nothing she could do about it.

"Do you want to come on my tongue, baby girl?"

"I…" She seemed to be gasping for air already. "Yes, please, Sir."

I licked all the way around her hot little entrance, enjoying her squirming. Then I concentrated on her clit while sliding two fingers deep into her pussy.

"Oh my god… Oh, fuck…" she moaned, twitching from

head to toe. "Darren… This is too much… I don't know if…"

"Breathe, Emma."

I rotated my hand so that the tips of my fingers were digging into her G spot with every slow thrust inside her.

"Do you want to come for me? Do you want to fill my mouth with your luscious pussy juices?"

I lapped hard at her sensitive button while she tried to form words.

"Mmm hmm," she moaned.

"I need to hear you say it, baby. You know I love it when you talk dirty. Please your Master, right now."

For once she didn't hesitate and gave me exactly what I commanded.

"Yes, Master, please… Make me come on your tongue. You're making me so wet. Please, don't stop licking my clit."

I increased my speed, lapping steadily while finger fucking her harder. Her strange moaning cry filled the air, and her thighs begin to quiver. The way she was opening herself to me so completely was incredibly sensual. Her hips tightened, and I gripped her ass with my free hand, giving her a little squeeze.

"Master!" she suddenly screeched, as her entire body began to tremble and the orgasm rolled through her. Her pussy was clenching around my fingers, and I continued licking hard until she became still.

Her breathing was ragged, her shoulder is twitching. I moved quickly so that I was beside her, so I could examine her eyes.

"Are you okay?"

"Yes," she grinned. That just feels so… Filthy, I guess. The way you were back there. I don't know. I felt so… Exposed."

I stroked her hair, and she actually tilted her head into

my hand. "If it would please Master, I'm so wet. All ready for your huge cock."

In a flash my shorts were on the floor and I was kneeling behind her. It was hard to be gentle as I eased inside her. At this angle it was a very, very tight squeeze.

"Can you handle the pressure in this position, baby?"

"I think so," she said.

Gripping her hips, I pressed deeper, adoring her tiny little moan. I worked into her slowly, knowing that everything was more intense at this angle. But she was pushing back against me, straining slightly as she wiggled her hips, trying to take me deeper.

"Don't hurt yourself, baby."

"But… Just a little… It feels so good."

"Careful." I released her hips and spread my hands across her shoulder blades, stroking gently. "I can't bear the thought of actually hurting you, sweetheart."

I wasn't sure whether I'd ever called her that before, or anyone, for that matter. My feelings for this breathtaking girl were becoming jumbled and messy.

"More, please, Sir," she breathed.

The way she was rocking back against my rigid shaft, working it deeper into her slippery soft pussy with every thrust, I couldn't stand the intensity of the pressure much longer.

Gripping her hip with one hand and reaching around to massage her clit with the other, I tried to fight the urge to be aggressive. Her shoulders were twitching as she moved, almost dancing under me as she worked her hips. I felt that indescribable tension in my balls, as my muscles tightened and everything began to flush with heat.

"Come for me, my perfect little angel," I growled, working a little faster, deeper as I try to steady her gyrating hips. Circling my fingers over her hot little clit, I saw that her shoulders were shaking harder.

"Yes… Sir… I just…"

"That's it, baby girl. Obey your Master. Let me control your body. Come all over my cock right now."

She screamed, her head flung back, pussy gushing as I felt myself slide deeper. "Oh fuck, Master, yes… Don't stop, harder… I need…" She screamed again, as her orgasm completely possessed her

I couldn't hold on, as her tight passage gripped me with her little spasms. "Emma," I choked, then I felt myself blasting her insides with the most forceful ejaculation of my life.

We rocked together, slowing down until I stopped, pulling out quickly and flipping her onto her back.

After checking that she was smiling and relaxed, I untied her legs quickly while openly staring at her gaping pussy, covered erotically in both of our juices.

Untying her wrists, I laid beside her while we both caught our breath. Then she reached out to hold my hand, causing my heart to surge.

*** THREAT OF THE CANE ***

What the hell was wrong with me? Every other submissive I had trained had been interested in learning what I had to teach. I was actually very good at rope ties and chain bondage. Coaching subs on how to kneel, walk, and always be on display for the Master was something I enjoyed.

But all Emma wanted was constant sex.

She was impossible to discipline, but it seemed like I was going to be the one who required the most work. I needed to get my raging libido under control so that I could bring this girl around. She'd been with me for almost a week, and the only submissive thing she'd learned was how to rip my pants off faster.

I had to find a way to make her want to behave. To establish a reward system, since the punishment wasn't working. Or… was it just that I'd only given her sexy punishments so far? Perhaps something more strict, with a reward within sight.

Bringing her into the playroom, she looked so cute – naked except for her collar.

"This is a very easy exercise, Emma," I said, looking directly into her eyes. "It's simply to teach poise and patience."

"Okay."

I shot her a look, tapping my foot.

"Oh, right, sorry. Okay, Sir."

"Emma, it's my job to teach you. You have to let me."

"Okay, Sir."

"Good girl. Now get on your knees."

She flashed me a smirk, dropping to her knees and opening her mouth as she raised her chin.

"Be serious. Mouth closed."

She shrugged. How could such a bright girl be such a

pain in the ass?

"Now pull your entire body up from your bum so that you are an inch taller than you thought you were. Visualize your lines." I took a piece of hair from the top of her head and gave it a tiny tug to help her feel it. She sat up a bit straighter.

"Good. What you're trying to do is create a beautiful picture for your Master to look at. Your hands sit gently on your thighs, your shoulders are slightly back and down so that your breasts look perky, and your chin is up but your eyes are down and soft."

She tried to do everything I requested, arranging herself appropriately.

"Your attention should always follow your Master, but your eyes remain in a neutral position in front of you."

Her eyes met mine with a little wink, then she gazed back at the floor.

"Good. Keep your eyes fixed in front and sort of keep an eye on me in your peripheral vision."

She seemed like she was trying to relax into the position.

"There you go. Perfect."

I walked over to my desk, picking up a timer. "For the first exercise you'll just have to hold that for five minutes. Ready?" She gave a tiny nod. I set the timer and placed it on the desk. "Go."

I sat down and picked up my phone, flipping through a couple of emails while watching her out of the corner of my eye.

Her attention began to wander after about a minute, and I saw her head turn to admire a huge green and gold painting filled with circles and rows of metallic bronze dots.

"Emma. Eyes front."

"Right. Sorry, Sir."

I shook my head. "We'll have to start again."

"Seriously?"

"Absolutely."

Resetting the timer, I set it on the desk with a bit of a click. "Go."

This time she made it almost two minutes before scratching her shoulder and looking around.

"Emma, do you still want to be my submissive?"

She looked up, surprised. "Yes, Sir."

"Emma, if you don't get it right this time, you'll be punished." Her eyes lit up with delight. "No, little girl, it won't be a spanking."

"Mmm, yes, Sir. Punish my mouth again."

"No. This time it will be the cane."

She barely looked worried, having only been spanked with my bare hand. Most submissives would shudder at the mere thought of the cane.

I walked to the rack on the wall, selecting a medium-sized cane. The long, slightly flexible stick didn't look particularly menacing, but the sting was incredible. "Hold out your hand."

Emma obeyed, looking curious. I gave her a tiny snap against her palm and she shrieked, wincing. Then she stared up at me in shock.

"That was perhaps five percent of the force I'll be using across your ass and hips unless you perform this one simple task perfectly. Do you want ten lashes?"

Her soft, sweet eyes looked up at me in horror, and I wanted to scoop her into my arms and swear to never hurt her. But she had signed up for a month of education. She had to learn at least a little bit, and most dominants would be far, far more strict than I was being.

"No, Sir," she whispered.

"Sit pretty."

Her spine lengthened as she pulled everything up through her core, her gaze softly three feet in front of her on the floor. Her fingers were close together, resting on the tops of her thighs. Perfectly motionless except for steady breathing, she looked like she could either stay there for hours, or jump up to serve her Master any second.

I set the timer again, setting it on the table, aimed away so that she couldn't see it. Sitting at the little desk that was occasionally used for school or office fantasies, I pulled out a bondage magazine and began reading, glancing at her occasionally.

This time she looked determined. About three minutes in, I saw her shoulders begin to twitch slightly, so I reached toward the cane sitting on the desk. She became perfectly motionless again, and I leaned back, skimming an article about conditioning jute rope with coconut oil.

Just before the timer sounded, I studied her. She seemed slightly agitated, but was remaining still. The bell rang. She still didn't move, but began to breathe a little more easily.

Turning it off, I stood up, walking to stand in front of her. Stroking her hair gently, I said, "Eyes." Emma looked up at me expectantly. "Good girl. I'm very proud of you."

Her little smile held something I hadn't seen before. I think she was proud of herself as well.

"Up."

She stood smoothly, gracefully, standing to face me while standing straight with her head raised.

"What do we do when we don't need our hands?" She nodded quickly, clasping them gently behind her back.

"Good girl."

Her tiny smile was so sweet, so sexy. It was absolute torture not to grab her and throw her across the desk, burying myself inside her. But we both needed to learn to control ourselves and play our parts.

"How do you feel?" I asked her gently.

"Fine, thank you, Sir."

It wasn't what she said, it was her tone. She was

expecting me to take her immediately. Instead, I walked over to the corner where there were three hard-points in the ceiling – huge metal rings with chains hanging from them.

"Have you ever been suspended, little one?"

"No, Sir." She actually sounded slightly nervous.

"Each one of those points can take five hundred pounds. You're not made of osmium or something, are you?"

She giggled, then pulled herself together immediately. "No, Sir."

"Spread your legs and stay still."

Her face lit up, then fell as I took a length of jute and tied a quick hip harness. Grabbing another, I tied a chest harness, then picked up a couple of carabiners.

I picked her up and threw her over my shoulder, loving her tiny squeal. Hooking the back of her hips onto a chain, I slowly slid her partway off so that only her shoulder was resting on me. Snapping the back of her chest harness onto a second chain, I eased her away gently so that she was floating face down. Apparently being on the front is easier for the first suspension, because falling forward is less terrifying than falling backward.

Quickly checking everything to make sure the pressure was even across every line, I tried not to think about what I could do to her while she was trussed up like this.

"Is anything uncomfortable?"

"No, Sir."

"How do you feel? Speak freely."

"I… it's…" She looked flustered.

I took one of her hands. "Deep slow breath. I'm right here. You're only four feet in the air."

Emma nodded. "Yeah. I know I'm safe, but the feeling that I could fall is freaking me out."

"Do you want me to take you down right now, or do you want to see if you can settle down for a minute?"

Her eyes met mine, and she seemed completely tense.

But then determination snuck in. "Give me a minute."

"Okay." I stroked her hair for a second, then stepped back.

She quickly reached out for my hand again, and I grabbed it. "Just… let me hold on."

"Okay, baby," I murmured. "Whatever you want." I knew by all accounts this was a completely gentle suspension, that every rope bunny said was perfectly comfortable. But everyone had a different reaction to new things.

"Think of yourself as a puppet that isn't being used at the moment," I joked. "Just breath, and hang gently."

She grinned, and I saw her chest and shoulders expand, then release. Her legs and free arm sagged, and she sunk into the ropes more naturally.

After a moment, she gave my hand a little squeeze, then released it. I stepped back, staying right in front of her so that I could grab her at any second.

She knew she was perfectly safe, but felt completely vulnerable. Our fear of falling runs deep, to a primal place hardwired in our brains. I knew that she understood I would never put her in any danger, but her instincts, her body, might not be able to accept that at first.

After several minutes of hanging quietly, I asked, "How do you feel now?"

"Weird," she said with a giggle. "Like I'm floating."

"Do you mean your body is floating, or you're getting a bit of an adrenaline high?"

"Both."

"I'm going to take you down in just a second, but first, do you want me to swing you?"

"Whatever you like, Sir."

I was impressed by her answer. Giving her shoulders a tiny push, I watched her tight little figure swing back and forth just a foot or so, while she giggled merrily.

I let her swing for about two minutes, then I stopped her. Putting her over my shoulder again, I held her tightly with one arm while unclipping her hips, then her shoulders. Lying her on the ground on her back, I began untying the ropes. She laid still at first, then began squirming slightly.

"What are you thinking about, little one?"

"I really like being your toy," she whispered, looking up at me with her saucy smile.

"Does that mean you want to be my good girl? From now on, I can only touch you if you behave."

She nodded, then made a face. "You wouldn't really have hit me with that stick thing, would you?"

"The cane. Yes, sweetie, I really would. If that's what it takes to teach you what you need to learn. I would give you a few sharp cracks so that the pain would sit with you for days. You'd have a nasty bruise, and be uncomfortable." I placed a finger under her chin. "Please, baby, don't make me do that. You know I don't want to."

I didn't want to break her spirit, but if she truly wanted to be a submissive, she had to make the decision either way.

*** ALL THE WAY ***

I always wondered if I would feel degraded, tied and owned by a dominant Master. Instead, I felt worshiped, as if I were the most precious thing in his entire world. It was overwhelming, this level of attention and care.

Studying Darren's eyes, I was torn. He wanted so desperately for me to behave, but he obviously adored it when I jumped him. Maybe there was a happy medium somewhere. I really did feel a deep need to submit to him. And perhaps if I played by the rules, he'd fuck me just as much.

"I'll try harder, Sir. I know we both don't want the cane."

He looked relieved.

"Baby, I think I know what I need to do with you."

"Yes?"

"If you don't behave, I'm not going to fuck you again."

I giggled, but then I saw how serious his eyes were. I'd rather take the cane than have him be this close to me and not let me take care of that wildly huge, perfect cock.

"I'll be good, Sir," I said quickly.

He finished untying the ropes, tossing them aside.

"Master," I said, looking up at him, "Did I behave like a good girl while you strung me up?"

"Yes, baby," he said, stroking my hair. I spread my legs wide, reaching up to pull his lips to mine. He didn't fight me, kissing me slow and deep. His warm mouth covering mine turned my brain off completely until I was running purely on instinct. I pulled him closer, on top of me, then reach down to rip off his shorts.

"Let me show you I can be your good girl. Let me show you I can take every punishment you need to give me."

He chuckled while shoving his shorts away. The way his eyes skimmed over my breasts, locking on my lips, drove me just as wild as the way he kissed me.

He slipped two fingers between my pussy lips, tracing back and forth as he opened me, then gently pressed inside.

"You're so wet," he murmured.

"My entire body wants you, Sir," I whispered without thinking.

Pulling his fingers out for just a second, he dipped his thumb into my juices, bringing it to my clit as his fingers dug back inside my slippery folds. The friction of his hand massaging me in two places at once filled me with waves of lust I couldn't begin to understand.

Even though I was lying on the carpeted floor, I felt like I was floating. I've never had anyone touch me so precisely, so carefully.

"I love the way you take control of my body, Sir." I heard myself whisper.

"I love the way you let me."

His lips circled my breasts in a long string of luscious open mouthed kisses, while I tried not to squirm under him. Then he wrapped his lips around my nipple, grazing his teeth carefully over the sensitive tip.

"Your delicious, baby." He nibbled harder, almost biting me.

"Oh fuck, oh yes," I blurted, squirming wildly.

"You like that, baby? You like a tiny bit of pain with your pleasure?"

"Yes… Yes, sir. More, please."

He bit my nipple carefully, listening to every little squeal and moan as his fingers worked faster.

"Harder, bite me… Make it hurt."

He switched to the other side, circling gently then suddenly giving me a sharp bite all the way around my peak. I screamed, coming instantly as I writhed helplessly under him. My breath was coming into ragged gasps and my vision was blurred as I thrashed against the floor, my limbs flailing helplessly.

Then I grabbed his face between my hands. "Fuck me, Master. Now. All of it."

The now-familiar feeling of the thick bulbous head of his cock sinking between my pussy lips filled me with joy, but this time the pressure inside was a bit less.

"Baby, you're so silky, so soft inside."

His arms scooped under my back, pulling me up against him as he slowly eased his thick monster of a cock inside me. This time I was so relaxed, so absolutely soaked, that he kept on going.

"Emma, is this too much?"

"I want all of you," I begged. "Please, own me completely, Master."

He cautiously pressed deeper, opening me slowly. The thrill of my body being stretched for him was almost making me high. I squirmed my hips a little, bucking against him, then suddenly I felt pressure at the very end of my tunnel. He was tapping against my cervix, and I gasped – so happy I could have cried.

He pulled back instantly. "No, don't stop," I begged. "That feels amazing. I'm just overwhelmed."

He took long, slow strokes very carefully, and as I looked up into his eyes I could see that he was already right on the edge.

"You love how tight my little pussy grips you, don't you, Master?"

He nodded, looking down at me with absolutely ferocious hunger.

"Does Master want to fuck his little girl hard?"

"Baby, I'm not going to risk hurting you," he smiled gently.

"Didn't you just see how hard I came because you were giving me a tiny bit of pain with the pleasure?"

"That's different. That was just a tiny bite."

"Please," I grabbed the back of his neck, working my fingers into the thick, dark hair. "Darren, I've never been this open with anyone. For anyone. In all possible ways. Please, I need you to fuck me hard. I swear it will only take a minute to make me come."

He looked at me strangely, then something seemed to release deep inside him.

His deep strokes became faster, harder, until he was pounding into me with a force that I couldn't quite believe. It was too much... But I could handle it. I wanted it so badly, and the pleasure was washing over me, putting me in a strange trance.

Pain mixed with pleasure has always been the naughtiest of all sensations, and this much devastating pleasure was making me scream and tremble to a degree but I thought I was losing my mind.

"More, more," I squealed, terrified that he might stop. Electricity was vibrating through every nerve, and I felt like I was going to actually explode. Each thrust of my new Master's gigantic cock stretching me open sent me closer to the edge.

Gripping his hair in both of my hands, I held his face in front of mine. Looking deeply into his eyes, I gasped, "Harder, Master... Make your pet come for you."

"Oh, baby," he murmured, his dark voice tight.

I looked directly into his eyes as I came hard, my mouth falling open as I choked for air, my fingers shaking as my entire body shook and thrashed under his.

*** EMMA'S LITTLE NOISES ***

Her choked squeal was so raw that it drove me insane.

I'd never been like this before. I'd never felt so raw, so uninhibited. Emma was turning me into a wild animal and I was almost ashamed to say that this is what I had been craving for my entire life.

Although I was afraid to hurt her, the needy desperation as she asked for it harder sent me over the edge. I didn't climax as much as I pounded, fucked... then poured myself into her... Flooding her with my pent up lust, my absolutely infinite desire for her.

Her raspy panting as she still held my gaze melted my heart completely.

"Are you mine?"

"Yes," she breathed.

"Yes, what?"

Those pretty little doll eyes looked up at me as she gave me her sauciest grin. "Yes, Master."

Hearing her say that made my entire soul sing in triumph.

Emma was a mess – her hair clinging to her face, flushed, panting, mascara smudged on one side. I've never seen anyone so beautiful in my life.

I was completely spent for a moment, then energized in a rush. Kissing her forehead, I saw that Emma looked shaken.

Quickly moving to the side, I held her in my arms. "Baby, are you okay?"

She nodded quickly. "I... Yes. I'm fine. Just rattled."

"Oh fuck. Baby, I'm sorry–"

"No," she said quickly, sitting up. "I've always dreamed of someone taking me that hard. That was..." She looked up at me dreamily. "Amazing. Intense." She rested her head on my chest. "Good, but can't speak for a minute."

She flashed me her saucy grin, her sparkling eyes blazing.

Snuggling her in my arms, I chuckled. "Well, at least I know how to shut up my little brat." She laughed so hard she snorted, the weird little noise making us both laugh.

I realized that I should use this as a teaching moment. "Emma, when you're obedient, when you're in the right headspace, I'm able to let go with you. I can only fuck good girls that hard. Do you understand?"

Her eyes blazed, as she nodded firmly.

Caressing her shoulder, I murmured, "Tomorrow we'll do some proper training, and you'll start with a video series I have that teaches you how to anticipate your Master's wishes, and shadow him when he walks you. Maybe I'll take you to a club and keep you on a leash. Would you like that?"

"Sure," she said sleepily.

"Sure, what?"

Emma looked confused, then giggled. "Sure, Master."

Rolling her slightly, I gave her ass a tiny playful smack. "As of tomorrow, strict discipline will begin. We'll review the rules properly. No distractions."

"Mmm hmm." She was already falling asleep in my arms, probably because she knew I wouldn't have the heart to wake her.

If I didn't find some self-control tomorrow, I might never gain the upper hand and actually be the dominant in this situation.

As I gently brushed her hair out of her face, watching her breathing become steady, I wasn't sure if I wanted to. Having her out of control, a sexy force of nature in my home, was awakening things I never knew I needed. This might be an incredible learning experience for both of us.

***

***

-

Perfecting Emma
(BDSM Training School Book #6)

*** PLAYROOM ***

Every time that I have trained a submissive, it has been someone who has wanted to learn. I have never had to deal with a brat before. But Emma is so sexy, so fiery, and so bloody crazy that she has forced me to change her training completely.

Usually a submissive wants to obey, and when they make a mistake, the punishment is more for pleasure than actual correction. The pain becomes a sensation play element that may or may not lead to the bedroom.

With Emma, the only way to get her to behave is the threat of no sex.

Although last week I had given her a tiny tap on the hand with a cane that packs a particularly painful sting, telling her that she would get several cracks across the ass if she didn't behave, I really don't think she believed that I would strike her with it.

And she was right. I just couldn't. I could spank her a bit harder than she enjoyed, but there was no way I could actually take an implement to her beautifully sensitive creamy skin. So my only option was to threaten to not touch her at all.

Once she saw that I was completely serious, she changed her attitude. When she obeyed perfectly and learned her lessons, she would be rewarded with whatever sexual activities we decided would be fun at the time. Or, and naturally that this was my favorite option, I could simply take her any way I liked. She loved it when I controlled her, as long as sex was involved. She just had no patience for cleaning, serving, or obeying anywhere else.

I was determined to tease her into submitting properly early this evening, as I called her into my basement playroom. She always called it the dungeon, and I think she liked the way it sounded medieval and dark. Almost dangerous. I would prefer to think of it as a playroom because I didn't want to be giving out punishments, only pleasure.

Emma tapped on the door, entering quietly, then kneeling in the center of the floor. Her back was straight, shoulders back and down, with hands clasped behind her. Her head was held high, with her eyes lowered, gazing at a spot several feet in front of her. When she wanted something, she behaved perfectly.

She looked positively luscious, wearing nothing but her little white leather collar, and posed exactly how I had instructed her.

I walked over, tussling her short blond hair. "Good girl. Are you ready to challenge yourself tonight?"

"Yes, Master," she said politely.

I could tell from the way her nipples were tightened into pretty little peaks that she was horny as hell and would obey beautifully to get what she wanted.

"So well behaved, my sweet little pet," I murmured, trailing my fingers along the back of her shoulder blades. "I think I would like to play with you today while you are totally silent. I will tell you when you are permitted to make noise again."

She looked up at me, her eyes tight with frustration, but she nodded, just mouthing the words, "Yes, Master."

"You know that you can always say your safeword loud and clear no matter what." She nodded with a little smile. I knew that she appreciated that I was always concerned with her safety first.

I walked over to the high bed, snapping my fingers. "Crawl to me, pet." She scurried quickly, always delighted to be anywhere near a bed with me.

"Up," I commanded, and she stood, quickly climbing up and kneeling in the center, facing me. Emma was so adorably cute when she was this eager, and I loved toying with her.

"Hands behind your back, just be still."

She obeyed immediately, and I was extremely relieved.

I reached into a drawer by the bedside table, pulling out two zip ties and a pair of wire cutters. She didn't see the cutters, and I slid them under a pillow. Before she could really see what I was doing, I fastened her hands to her ankles on either side. It wasn't tight, but the hard plastic against the skin is unsettling.

Holding her face in my hands, I could see the terror washing through her as she squirmed slightly, testing the bonds behind her that she couldn't quite see properly.

"Breathe, baby. You know I would never hurt you. You know I could get you out of this in two seconds."

She nodded, taking a moment to try to calm herself. She was obviously twitchy, and her lips were tight. I let my hand run around her neck, her ear, the top of her shoulder.

"The lesson here, baby, is to force yourself to be calm in an uncomfortable situation."

She nodded, but she was obviously on edge. Not being able to speak to me was one thing. But the lack of communication while having her hands behind her, holding her open and vulnerable, was unnerving and unnatural.

My head dropped to swirl my lips around one nipple, then the other. Emma calmed down, her breathing becoming steady again.

Rolling her onto her back, her arms were straight on the bed, her knees bent and falling apart wide so that she was completely spread open for me. Emma's grin lit up her beautiful face. She thought I was about to fuck her now.

Her sweet peach of a pussy was already aroused, slightly swollen, slightly wet, as if she had been thinking about sex for hours. Her clit was practically standing at attention, begging for something, anything to brush across it. She was squirming slightly, anxious to have my hands on her, hungry for my touch.

Having this gorgeous girl so aroused for me was intoxicating, and I felt my cock positively throbbing against the thin fabric of my shorts. Once again I was both amused and annoyed at how her bratty tendencies have forced me to use a lot more self-control and discipline than her.

Her hips were beginning to wiggle back and forth, and I heard a faint little noise that was almost a whine emanating from her throat.

Resting my hands on her knees, applying just enough pressure to make her feel almost obscenely spread open, I asked, "Do the ties hurt, or can you handle that for twenty minutes?"

She nodded and gave me a little grin.

"Good girl," I said, then I leaned in quickly, bringing my mouth to her inner pussy lips. I licked, sucked, kissed her hard for about thirty seconds while she shook from head to toe at the shock.

Then I stood up straight, licking my lips. "Delicious, my sweet pet."

Her breath was coming in rattling gasps, and her soft little pussy was so wet she was beginning to drip onto the bed below. Emma's expressive eyes were looking up at me in a frantic blend of curiosity, arousal, and earnest begging.

"You have a choice now, sweet baby girl." She nodded eagerly.

"I can snip your ties and you can go to your room for the rest of the night." Her nose crinkled up as she shook her head.

"Or, you can practice being perfectly still for me for twenty minutes, then I'll give you a quick handjob and send you to bed."

Her lips pressed into a line as she shot me a slightly irritated look, as if to say, "Get to the good stuff."

"Or I can slip a tiny butt plug into your ass and see if you like it."

Her mouth fell open as she made a squeaking noise, then she snapped it shut. We had never done any anal play before, but she had always been open to everything.

She looked at me with a saucy grin, then nodded.

"Good girl. You know that I'll be careful with you."

She nodded again.

I'm not sure why it was such a perverse little thrill, but I loved it when women wore a butt plug for me. It was so filthy, such a sick little thrill. Emma's ass was so round, tight, and deliciously perfect. I knew that it might not work given my size, but taking her that way would be heaven.

Pulling a small pink plug out of its package from the drawer, I also pulled out a bottle of lube, coating the toy carefully along with my finger.

"Just relax, baby," I said gently, placing my finger against her entrance without pressing inside.

I made slow circles around her tight little rosebud, pressing against it gently while she trembled under me. Leaning in, I began nuzzling her mound, licking along her outer pussy lips as the softest moan filled the room. Pressing inside her very slowly, I worked my finger in while I lapped at her hot little pussy.

She seemed a little nervous at first but was obviously trying to relax for me.

It seemed like she needed a few minutes to get used to the pressure. A little tremor went through her, and my finger slipped deeper.

*** INSERTION ***

There were so many things that I had never done before, but I was open to exploring with Darren. Yet I was extremely nervous about this. I did want to open myself to him completely. The sensation of him owning my body and using it any way he liked was overpowering.

The more I relaxed, the more his finger slipped deeper, gently wiggling inside. The pressure was weird, but it was also deliciously naughty.

His hot tongue was working eagerly against my clit, and I found myself surrendering to every feeling that flowed through me. A tiny low murmur rang through my throat before I could stop it.

"Silent, baby. You can do it."

I nodded, trying to slow my breathing and relax.

His thick finger slowly slid all the way out of my tight tunnel, then I sensed him reaching for something. A chilly wet point pressed against my tight hole, and he began pushing very slowly.

He began thrusting his tongue into my pussy in time with his tiny thrusts with the butt plug. Rocking in gradually, I adored his patience with me.

I needed to grab his hair, his shoulders, let him know how much I enjoyed his attention. But having me spread open and helpless obviously excited him. I envisioned him fucking me in this position, his body spread over mine while I was pinned, captured.

As his tongue began to caress my clit again, I imagined his thick shaft entering me, and my entire body welcomed him in. The butt plug slipped inside me completely, and as he gave it a little twirl, his tongue bore down on my swollen nub of nerves.

The climax flowed through me like a tiny prickle of sparkles that became an explosion. My mouth fell open and

I gasped, silently screaming while I convulsed under him. I felt my juices flooding his tongue and mouth, while I tried not to let my hips squirm.

"Good girl," he said, kissing my inner thigh. He looked up, and I realized how proud he was of me.

"Wiggle your wrists. Is anything digging into you?" I shook my head.

He flipped me over so that I was on my front, so there was absolutely no pressure on my wrists and ankles.

Glancing at him over my shoulder, he was staring at my ass. "Baby, I wish you could see how fucking hot this looks."

He spread my cheeks gently, admiring the little plug tucked inside me. Pressing my lips together hard, he saw my shoulders twitch as I stifled a giggle.

Coming beside me and leaning in, he kissed me gently, with that sultry fire that I always felt from him during our playtime. His tongue slipped into my mouth to glide against mine. This time I couldn't stop my soft little moan, but it seemed to amuse him.

"You can make all the noise you like now, baby," he said.

"Thank you, Master," I whispered.

He quickly unclipped the ties so that I could stretch out on the bed. My entire body was still tingling from the amazing rush.

"My gorgeous sweet little pet, it's time for you to do some chores."

I tried not to roll my eyes at him, looking at him expectantly. "Yes, Master?"

"If you would like me to play with you again with that plug in, you could sweep the floor, and dust this room. Supplies are in the cupboard."

He gave me a little kiss, then left the room, calling out, "I'll be back in an hour."

My natural tendency was to ignore his request, and just jump him when he came back in. I knew how much he loved fucking me, and that it was extremely hard for him to resist.

On the other hand, seeing how happy he was when I made him proud was fascinating. I never had a man be proud of me before. I never wanted to please anyone this badly.

I got up and stretched for a minute, remembering how he had told me to stay limber so that weird bondage positions would never harm me.

Going to the closet and getting the supplies, I swept the entire playroom, then dusted, then used the glass cleaner and rags to polish the giant mirror that took up half of the wall near the bed. By the time Darren returned, the room was spotless and I was kneeling in the center of the floor just the way he liked. It was tricky not to squirm from the pressure deep inside me.

He looked around the entire room, almost doing a double-take when he saw the spotless mirror. The feeling of his huge hand ruffling my hair filled me with pride. "Good girl," he said gently. "Such a sweet little pet to obey her Master so perfectly."

Smiling up at him with my eyes wide, I couldn't wait for him to touch me again.

"Sweetheart, does the plug feel okay?"

I nodded.

"You're completely comfortable with it?"

"Yes, Master. I mean, it's a little weird, and when I'm moving around, it makes it impossible to think about anything but sex."

He grinned at me. "That's the point."

Then he cocked his head, his deep eyes looking at me with genuine curiosity. "Baby, I know you are incredibly tight, but do you think you would like me to try to fuck you with that thing in?"

"I... I don't know." Then I grinned. "Yes."

"Do you think you'd like me to take the plug out and replace it with my cock?"

I bit my bottom lip. "I think… I think I might like to try?"

His smile sent tingles running through me. "That's my good girl. I love that you are so willing to try."

He dropped his shorts, snapping his finger and pointing to the center of the bed. I was giddy with excitement as I rushed over and laid across the sheet, spreading my legs for him.

"I've been missing your pussy all day, baby. Let's try that first." I nodded eagerly.

He reached into the table drawer for the bottle of lube, coating his erection with it. I loved how quickly he got hard for me without me even touching him. It was strangely erotic that all he had to do is glance in my direction and his body prepared itself.

Staring down at me, his gaze drank me in, and I squirmed underneath him.

"I was going to eat your rosy pink pussy until you scream, but seeing you with that thing in your hot little ass I just can't wait…" He began rubbing his huge thick head across my pussy lips, and I moaned, my legs splaying wider for him.

"That's okay, Master… I want to feel you."

He leaned in, kissing my forehead. "I adore how much you always want me, baby."

Pressing his huge shaft into me slowly, the delicious sensation of being filled made me gasp and moan. The pressure of his cock pushing against the butt plug filling my other tunnel was strange.

"Is that too much, baby?"

I shook my head. "It's a lot, but I think I like it."

He kissed me hard, that creeping fire between us always surprising me with its intensity. I loved that his lips ravaged mine while his cock was incredibly slow and gentle.

My tender pussy stretched open for him gradually until he filled me completely. It felt like my insides were straining, the tension building as he began taking long, slow strokes.

Since I was always so wet for him, he had never used lube to enter my pussy before. It was amazing, as I really felt his skin slipping against my clit with every stroke.

Wrapping my legs around his waist and my arms around his shoulders, I clung to him, loving his skin against mine. His hands were everywhere – groping my breasts, gripping my waist, and stroking the back of my shoulders. The way he fondled me, enjoying my body as his toy made my pulse quicken.

Darren's strokes became faster, slightly deeper, as he shoved his huge cock into me, moving against the firm plug. My shoulders quivered as the knot in the center of my belly began to deepen, the tension building. It felt like I was about to explode at any second.

"Don't come," he ordered.

I looked up at him and heard myself whine, "Why?"

He stopped moving completely and I could have cried from frustration. "Why, what?" he asked teasingly.

"Why, Master?" I said quickly, nearly panting with desire.

"Because I said so."

"Please, you feel so good, Master," I begged.

He resumed fucking me deeply, slowly. "This is my pretty little pussy, and I want it to wait."

Darren's lips took mine again as he began thrusting harder, faster. My tiny whimpers seemed loud, but the sound of his cock wetly grinding into my pussy lips was the more seductive noise.

"Master, may I please come for you now?"

"Not yet."

I was torn between needing to climax but trying to obey him. He seemed so determined to control me. Why was it so hard for me to give in to what we both wanted?

Taking a long, slow breath, I tried to calm myself. Relax. Surrender. "Okay, Master. Whatever you wish."

His eyes fixed on mine, blazing with joy. "That's my girl."

"Yes, Master. Yours."

He untangled our bodies so that I was flat on my back, and he laid my hands at my sides. Grabbing my legs, he threw them over his shoulders so that my ass was slightly lifted. Then he took my hands, setting them on the outside of his thighs so that I could hold on.

He was so unbelievably deep at this angle that I was overwhelmed by the pressure. But he was no longer rubbing against my clit, so now it would be easier for me to hold off my climax. Probably.

He gripped my waist, his hips rocking toward me again and again in an undulating wave. I adored the way he didn't just ram his cock into me. He used it to explore my reactions. With every stroke he penetrated me slightly differently, touching different nerves, experimenting. Every tiny gasp and moan was a signal to him of how intense it was for me.

I had never even imagined being with a man who was this creative, this expressive, this exploratory.

This level of attention was making me feel altered. As if I were outside of myself looking in. Even though I was somehow completely grounded in my body, I was floating.

Digging my fingers into his skin, I pulled against him a few times, lifting my pelvis a bit more to force us together. Feeling the way his thickness throbbed inside me, I realized I was looking forward to his climax more than my own. I wanted to feel him lose himself inside me.

Looking up into those gorgeous, deep eyes, he reached

out to caress my cheek, smiling gently.

A tremor ran through me. Dammit. I was in love with him.

But not just that – I was in love with the way he made me feel. Made me think. He made me question and explore and analyze things about myself that I had never even thought of before. As much as I loved him, I was in love with the version of myself that he was bringing out into the open.

Tears pricked the corners of my eyes at this revelation, and my chest became tight as the air I was breathing suddenly felt too thick.

He noticed immediately, pulling out and lowering my legs. "Baby, what's wrong?"

I tried to smile, but it felt like every part of me was shaky.

"What can I do, baby?" he begged, his eyes burning into mine. He was instantly so desperate to take care of me that it touched me even more, and I had to swallow hard before I could find my voice. "I'm fine, Master. Really. Just… Suddenly overwhelmed."

He exhaled hard. "Thank Christ. I thought I hurt you, baby."

"Please, don't stop," I begged, looking up at him. "It felt so good. I'm sorry that I–"

He dragged his thumb against my lips as he slowly put my legs over his shoulders again. "Never apologize for being expressive and honest, Emma. I love that about you."

My breath hitched again, deep in my lungs as I saw him realize what he had just said.

"Please keep going," I said softly, taking a breath before quickly adding, "Master."

Feeling him slowly slide back into my tight, wet pussy was so powerful I had to blink hard to stop my eyes from tearing up again. Gripping his thighs tightly, I leaned my shoulders back, arching slightly so that he could lift my ass and enjoy me at any angle he liked.

"You're so soft, baby."

His deep, powerful strokes now felt possessive. As much as we were sharing these feelings together, my blood was boiling from the knowledge that he was also taking me. I was his to enjoy, and he knew it. I was offering myself to him completely.

He leaned down and cradled the back of my head in his hand as he raised my lips to his. Bringing his thumb to my mouth, he pulled away so that I could suck on it for a moment. Seeing how amused he was by my giggling made me laugh even harder.

He brought his slippery thumb to my clit as he kissed me again. Running little circles all around the surface without quite touching it fully, he teased me while stroking gently inside me.

The feeling of the plug in my ass was creating a weird tension that I was still trying to process, but in the spirit of giving myself to him, I now knew what I wanted.

I broke our kiss just long enough to murmur, "Master, if it should please you, please take my ass tomorrow."

He answered by kissing me deeply, his thumb caressing me more firmly as the friction of his thick cock increased with every stroke.

My heartbeat was ringing through my ears and my energy gathered, just one step away from the edge. Concentrating hard on not climaxing divided my attention, allowing me to focus on him. Pulling my muscles inward, I tried to massage his shaft by gripping him harder with my pussy walls.

"Oh fuck," he groaned against my mouth. "Emma, that's incredible."

Making Darren lose control was somehow intimate, erotic. I was usually needy, anxious for my own climax. But this time, all I wanted was to feel him release deep inside me.

"Does this please my sexy Master?" I asked sweetly, fluttering my eyelashes as I concentrated harder on working my muscles around him.

"It does, very much. Does my sweet baby want to come for me now?" I nodded, looking up at him hopefully.

He began thrusting harder, rocking his length into me almost aggressively, as his thumb swirled directly against my sensitive clit.

"Come for me, pretty little pet," he commanded.

His dark tone pushed me over the edge, tumbling and shrieking as I thrashed between him and the bed. He stared deeply into my eyes while I quivered, as if he were completely entranced by watching me lose my mind for a few moments. The rush of pure sensation was magical.

"I can't believe how sexy you are when you let go completely," he said gently, his body still pounding into mine.

Realizing that he was on the verge as well, I couldn't stop wiggling up against him.

"Fill me, Master," I begged him brazenly. "I want to feel you come inside me. Come deep. Please... Your little pet needs it so bad." He gave in with a deep growl, drenching the inside of my pussy with his hot juices. "Yes," I squealed. "Thank you, Master."

His deep quick strokes became gentle, languid, almost soothing. His thumb continued to massage my clit gently. His lips raised into a sideways smile.

"Your Master wants to watch you come again."

Feeling how much he enjoyed my pleasure sent me back to the edge in seconds. Even though his cock had softened slightly, it was still pressing against the butt plug, still filling me almost completely.

The heavenly sweet way he was stroking deep into my

gushing passage was intoxicating. This climax almost snuck up on me, hitting me with a shock as the sparkling waves washed over me and I squealed, trembling and tingling.

"My good girl," he murmured. He gently set me down and pulled out, rolling me over onto my stomach.

Stroking my back gently, he asked, "Are you ready for me to take the plug out?"

"Yes, Master," I whispered, looking over my shoulder at him and giving my ass a little shake.

Darren laughed, giving me a tiny spank, then pulling the toy out very gently. I expected to feel relief once it was gone, but instead I felt momentarily empty.

He laid on the bed while I snuggled up into his shoulder. "Do you really want me to try to fuck your sexy ass tomorrow?"

"Yes, Master."

Placing a finger under my chin, he tipped my face up so he could read my expression. "Do you want to talk about what made you feel overwhelmed?"

Closing my eyes quickly, I shook my head. Although I knew that he truly cared for me, I didn't know how deep it ran, or whether he would even allow himself to love a submissive who wasn't as into the theory and protocol of BDSM as he was. I also didn't even know if he was looking for a more permanent partner. I just couldn't think about that right now.

"Okay," he said softly, kissing my hair. "I'm always ready to listen. You don't have to share if you don't want to, but you know I want to know everything about you."

I nodded, my face buried against his chest.

"You're amazing, Emma. I hope that you truly understand that."

He rocked me to sleep in his arms, and I drifted off in complete bliss.

*** TRYING ***

Waking up in my own bed, I was momentarily startled. How on earth had he carried me upstairs, tucked me in, and pulled blankets over my naked body without me waking up? And how did I manage to sleep in this late?

I took a few moments to stretch, making sure that I wasn't stiff from yesterday's ties. One thing about bondage is that it's easy to hurt yourself from pulling against the restraints, but I've been learning to try to stay loose.

When I went to the kitchen to make coffee, there was a note on the table.

Sweet little girl, I'm sorry I had to go into the shop for several hours. I'll be back around three. If you need to stretch and rest today, that's fine. But if you have the energy to be an extra good pet, the kitchen could be cleaned for a bit, and here is a book on the psychology of BDSM. I think chapter four might be interesting to you.

xoxo

Even though he had given me the go-ahead to rest, I was overwhelmed with the need to please him.

I showered quickly, then grabbed my tablet. Sure enough, the book he wanted me to read was available as an audio-book. I was able to listen to chapters three and four while doing the dishes, scrubbing the counters, wiping down the cabinets, washing out the produce drawers in the refrigerator, and sweeping the floor.

Darren was absolutely right – the book was incredibly interesting. It explained how surrendering one's power to another for a short time doesn't make you weak. In fact, it makes you open, strong, and able to better bond with that person.

My resistance to obedience had nothing to do with

Darren. I simply had some weird glitches about obeying a man.

Perhaps it was because my mother was a vicious feminist, to the point of being angry all the time. But it should be about choice. If I choose to kneel at someone's feet for an hour, that doesn't mean that I won't stand up for myself at other times. I'm still completely capable of driving a truck, using power tools, being a strong woman however I see fit.

In fact, releasing all of my own wants and needs to give myself to another felt strangely calming. Almost like meditation. I became nothing but my breathing, and my service.

Laughing as I scrubbed the sink so hard it shone, I realized that this month of being a pet was exactly what it took to make me fully understand.

The second I heard Darren's bike in the driveway, I put the cleaning supplies away and knelt at the entrance to the kitchen, so he would see me as soon as he walked in the front door.

Fluffing up my hair and giving my cheeks a pinch to make them rosy, I realized I had forgotten to turn off the audio-book. Dammit.

He came in to hear the voice of the psychologist going on about limits, and how pushing one's limits carefully helps us to grow in ways far beyond the bedroom or the dungeon. It helps us grow as people and be open to new opportunities at all times.

"Baby, what are you listening to?"

"The book you suggested, Master."

He saw my tablet on the kitchen counter and hit pause. Then he looked around the room and saw I had cleaned from top to bottom. "Baby, you did all this?"

"And the inside of the fridge, Master."

Darren looked genuinely touched. "And you

downloaded the book so that you could listen to while you worked?"

I nodded, smiling up at him. He snapped his fingers, and I jumped up into his arms as he snuggled me close.

"My sweet little pet, what a good girl."

I found myself absolutely basking in his praise, feeling utterly satisfied. He scooped me up, taking me to the living room couch and cuddling me into his lap. Leaning into his chest, I felt like his darling pet more than ever.

"How was your day, Sir? Did everything turn out all right?"

He gave me a deep kiss that made my thighs tighten before answering. "Yeah. There was an old school chopper that one of our best clients wanted us to fix up so his friend's band could use it for a video shoot. It was an all hands on deck situation to get it done in time, and I was the only one who has really worked on this bike before."

I grinned up at him. "You seem like a very hard worker. I'm glad that it all turned out well for you."

He snuggled me into his shoulder, rocking me gently. It was a truly perfect moment, of my Master coming home to greet me after we both had a productive day of work. It made me wonder what would happen if we were together longer.

His shoulder smelled of his deep earthy scent, and I felt my reaction immediately. My body began pressing into him and I couldn't quite control it.

*** OBEDIENCE ***

I almost couldn't believe that my sweet little brat, the girl who wanted me to spoil her yet defied me at every turn, was finally coming around.

I knew that I should reward her good behavior, but somehow simply taking her to the playroom and fucking her senseless wasn't good enough. I wanted to reward her properly. To lavish her with attention and pleasure so she could understand how much I appreciated her new attitude.

"Are you tired after all of your cleaning?"

She shook her head, looking up at me with a seductive smile that definitely made my heart rate increase.

"Then come with me." I set her on her feet, and she followed me downstairs to the playroom.

Lifting her by the waist, I threw her into the center of the bed on her back. She giggled, then spread out like a starfish, ready for anything I wanted to do with her.

Grabbing the restraints from the drawer under the bed, I wrapped her wrists in soft leather cuffs, placing her hands together, attached to chains in the center of the headboard. She had room to move around a bit, but not much.

Then I took her ankles, latching them into leather cuffs as well, and connecting them to a spreader bar that I hung from the ceiling. The bar telescoped open to whatever width I liked, but I started with it extended just three feet.

Pulling off my work clothes, I dumped them in a heap on the floor, crawling naked into bed with her. She was looking at me expectantly as if she were ready for anything.

I leaned in to her lips, but then changed direction at the last second and lowered my mouth to her soft flat belly.

Sucking firmly, I created a trail of little pink marks that would likely fade within the hour. Emma looked down with amusement. "Are you branding me? Are you marking your territory?"

I looked up at her, then gave her inner thigh a slap. "What did we forget, pet?"

"Dammit. Sorry. Are you marking your territory, Master?"

Spinning the spreader bar, I flipped her so that she was on her front. "Now I see why you tied me up like this, Master. Clever."

I caressed of the silky skin of her curves, massaging her hips, ass and outer thighs. "Do you know why you must address me properly, my lovely pet?"

She turned back to look at me with a dreamy glow in her eyes. "So I never forget for one second that I belong to you, Master."

I could see that she was falling under the spell already. Not just playing the part of my toy, but learning to truly revel in it.

"That's right, baby. How many spanks do you think you deserve for forgetting?"

Her hips begin to wriggle, her excitement radiating through her skin. "As many as Master would like to offer me."

Somehow she was pushing all of my buttons, and I was so relieved at her change in attitude.

"Five, I think. Count them out, my sweet pet."

Giving her a sharp smack on the lower curve of her ass, she squealed in pleasure, calling out, "One, Master," in a singsong voice. With each spank, she responded loud and clear until she was done.

But now she couldn't seem to stop squirming, a tiny moan escaping her, and I realized I could not wait to enjoy her any longer. I could feel how much the spanking aroused her.

Flipping her onto her back again, I checked all of her cuffs to make sure they weren't too tight, then spread her legs wider.

Leaning in, I pinned her completely with my body, giving her a kiss so deep it consumed both of us. The breathless little whimper that escaped her lips was pure pleasure.

Feeling her submit to me like this filled me with the strange dominant energy I've always craved. Having her understand that whether I was spanking or caressing, it came from the same place of needing her to be completely mine.

The sweet warmth of her lips burned through me, and I realized that I needed to keep her. I couldn't stop being with her just because the calendar flipped a page. She's mine now, but we belonged to each other.

Gripping the back of her hair in my fist, I gently turned her chin up, kissing along her jaw, her throat, her collarbone. The way her breath halted and hitched thrilled me.

Kissing along to her luscious breasts, I circled in lazy figure eights, caressing with my hands and worshiping with my mouth. Her eyes were half shut as she arched her back slightly, offering herself to me.

I reached down to slip a hand between her legs, slowly sliding one finger into her soft pussy, delighted that she was already juicy and warm.

It felt like all of my blood rushed to my cock, leaving me nothing to think about beyond devouring this gorgeous creature.

Kneeling between her captive thighs, I slid a second finger inside her, stroking in and out slowly. Her hot little cunt gripped them snuggly, craving the feeling of being filled. Having her so open and juicy and ready for me made me need to fuck her senseless immediately, but I greedily needed to hear her come first.

Reaching up with my free hand, I rolled my fingers over her nipples, squeezing gently just to hear her tiny squeals. I leaned in to breathe her sweet scent, then slid my tongue over the top of her wet slit. Dragging it upward in long, luxurious strokes, I lapped steadily while she squirmed and moaned.

Her delicious honey was coating my lips and I just couldn't get enough. Giving her nipple one last pinch, I lowered my hand to her hip bone, holding her down while fucking her harder with my fingers.

Her little whimpers were driving me insane, and I flipped my tongue flat across her clit for a few minutes before sucking it into my mouth. I begin humming softly, the vibrations overtaking her. I could see her entire body trembling, and I loved that I was able to do this for her. With her.

"Does my lovely little pet want to come on my tongue?"

"Please... yes, Master."

I paused for another few moments, reveling in the feeling of her body quaking under my touch. Moving my fingers faster, deeper, I commanded, "Come for me now."

Flattening my tongue against her clit, I licked steadily upward as she crumbled to pieces, screaming while rattling the chains. It took me a second to realize there were words in her shrieks, as she yelped, "Thank you, Master," over and over.

When she finally stilled, I looked up at her with a grin, licking off my fingers and coming around to lie beside her, propped up on my elbow. I placed my hand in the center of her stomach, letting the weight calm her down.

"How do you feel, baby?"

"Amazing, Master," she murmured. The way she looked at me made my guts flip.

"Are you mine?" I asked. I meant it playfully, but the woozy look in her eyes made me realize how serious she was when she answered.

"Completely, Master."

My mouth found hers and I was kissing her deeply before I even realized it.

She was so warm, so ripe, that my body took over completely. Kneeling up for a second to open the spreader bar another two inches, she wiggled her legs slightly, knowing what was coming next.

Placing the thick, swollen head of my cock against her tiny pink lips, my pre-cum blended with her sweet juices as I eased inside her. She trembled, her hips moving gently as she tried to pull me deeper.

"That's it, my sweet little toy. Open up."

Emma's wrists pulled against the cuffs, not to escape, but because it was killing her not to throw her arms around me.

Winding an arm behind her shoulders, I tipped her up slightly as my cock sunk inside her inch by inch until I had bottomed out completely.

"My sweet good girl can take it all now," I grinned, and she nodded eagerly, leaning up to kiss me hard.

"I love how much your body wants me," I murmured, then her soft lips opened for me and I captured her darting tongue.

We moved together, rocking slow but deep, her sweet hips rolling beneath me. It felt like her hot pussy was milking my shaft, the pressure incredible. Lowering my teeth to her nipple, I scraped against her sensitive skin just enough to make her squeal.

Driving into her again and again, I could feel that she was near the edge already.

Bringing my thumb to her mouth, she grinned so sweetly as she sucked at it calmly knowing what was next. I slid it down to her clit, loving the way her eyes lit up. Pumping faster, deeper into her hot, tight pussy, I massaged her sweet little button while she quivered and moaned.

Then her eyes went wide, and her breathing hitched strangely. I realize she was trying hard not to come.

"Such a good girl," I murmured, easing off with my

hand while pounding her harder. "Does my pretty baby want to come?"

She nodded quickly, her breath still stuttering.

"You've been such a good girl today," I murmured, kissing her forehead. Then I looked deep into her eyes as I whispered, "Come for me, gorgeous."

Digging in more firmly with my thumb, I swirled harder while fucking her as if to break her. The intensity of her gaze burning into me was wild.

I could feel the quivering begin deep in her slick, tight pussy, radiating outward until her entire body was quivering while she screamed, her lips inches from mine as she let everything go.

When her mouth finally closed, her cheeks were flushed, and a crazy grin took over her pouty lips. "Wow," she giggled. "May I touch you now, Master?"

"Not yet, baby."

I reached up to snap the spreader bar back together so her ankles were only three inches apart. Throwing both of her legs over one shoulder, she twisted slightly with her thighs together. Plunging back inside her heavenly pussy, she was now even tighter. Watching her eyes carefully as the intensity washed over her, she looked up to give me a little nod, letting me know it was okay.

Stroking deep and quick, I felt both my blood and my balls boiling as I fucked her almost ruthlessly.

"Yes," she gasped. "Oh, my fuck… Yes, Master."

Grinding into her tight wet cunt, I gripped her around the waist, pinning her so that she was still while I thrust faster. Her little shrieks and cries echoed off the walls, and I could hear the soft slick sound of my cock taking her deep, over and over.

"You're so perfect, baby girl," I groaned. "Emma, tell me what you want."

"Come inside me," she begged. "Fill me up, Master.

Make my pussy drip for you. I need to feel you explode inside me."

That was the last straw, her dirty talk always undoing me completely.

I used every inch to pound her hard as I throbbed inside her, pumping rope after rope of thick, deep cum into her hot little passage. She whimpered, her whole body shuddering as if she were coming again.

I stayed still for a moment, feeling drained and fuzzy, then slowly eased out, holding her legs tightly as I uncuffed her.

Stroking her hair, I leaned in to give her a little kiss. "Too much?"

"Never, Master," she grinned, her eyes gleaming.

Unfastening her wrists, she threw her arms around me, holding me tight while she trembled. "That was amazing," she whispered. "Thank you, Master. "

I felt like I was high, this moment so perfect I couldn't believe it. Then I remembered what I was going to be doing in a few hours, and a shudder ran through me as I held her tight.

*** TOTAL SURRENDER ***

Darren sent me to my room to rest for a bit, but it was hard not to be super excited by what would be coming next.

It was funny, but I wasn't scared. I was more excited than nervous. I knew how much giving myself completely to him would excite him, and I wanted to please him above all else.

When Darren called me down to the playroom, I was already twitching with anticipation.

He didn't even let me kneel in front of him, just wrapped his arms around me while he kissed me, the heat between us instant and overwhelming.

"Do you still want to try this, baby?"

"Yes. Absolutely, Master."

He grabbed my chin, tilting my face up. "But you are going to stop and tell me before it hurts, not after. Right?"

"I promise, Sir."

He laid me on the bed, and I was a bit surprised he didn't restrain me in any way. Laying beside me, he kissed me gently, his hands running over my skin, warming up my nervous system to let him take over me.

"I love the way you touch me, Master," I murmured into his mouth.

"Then I guess I'll never stop touching you," he chuckled, kissing along my cheek to my ear lobe, nibbling gently.

His hand slid down my stomach, then lower as I automatically spread my legs for him. His thick fingers danced along my outer pussy lips, teasing me. I loved it when he was completely focused on me, watching every reaction from my body, and my eyes.

Spreading open my pussy, he circled one finger around my inner lips, dipping in slightly as I begin to squirm and moan for him.

"So sexy," he said, looking deeply into my eyes as he pressed his finger inside. The little whine that escaped my throat didn't even sound like me, but I didn't care. I couldn't censor myself around him. I was completely open, shameless, raw.

Darren kissed my nose, then moved between my legs, surprising me with an open mouthed kiss in the center of my pussy.

"Oh!" I moaned softly.

He spread my legs a bit wider, kissing me again, covering my pussy lips with his mouth as his tongue glided everywhere. Once I was a quivering puddle, he began tracing my slit in long, careful strokes.

It felt like every inch of me was opening, swelling, begging for more. As he latched his lips around my sensitive little button, I cried out without meaning to.

He stopped, looking up at me with eyes half-lidded from lust. "Who's pussy is this?"

"Yours, Master. Completely yours."

"Good," he growled, then he dug in again, licking my clit hard as he spread my outer lips with his thumbs, before sliding two fingers inside me.

My hands dug into his hair, as my hips shifted, pressing myself against him. "Yes…" I moaned, right on the edge. "Master, may I come?"

He answered by digging in harder, his tongue pressing deeply into my clit as his fingers pistoned in and out of my dripping twat. His free hand gripped my belly, his fingers digging and slightly as he clutched me, both holding me still and controlling my body.

It started as a slow burn, then washed over me as it gathered strength. This climax glided through my nerves like liquid fire as I gasped, squealing and moaning as my fingers dug into his scalp.

When I finally caught my breath, I released his hair,

stroking gently. "Sorry," I whispered.

He looked up at me and licked his lips. "You are so delicious."

Reaching into the drawer, he pulled out the bottle of lube, coating two fingers in the slippery gel. "I'm just going to get things started, okay?"

I nodded, then laid back and tried to relax. He began circling with just the tip of the finger, spreading the gel before pressing slightly inside.

He leaned in to circle my swollen clit with his tongue again and I found myself relaxing more. I barely noticed as his finger entered me at least an inch. My entire body was tingling for him, and I wanted to pull him inside me, no matter where he wanted to go.

Slowly, delicately, he lapped at my clit as his finger completely entered me, and was then joined by a second. Circling his fingers slightly, he opened my tunnel so gradually that it felt completely natural.

He sucked hard at my clit for a moment, then looked up at me with a grin. "Let's give this a try, my sweet baby."

I loved it when he called me that, and it made me want to prove myself to him even more.

Darren came up and sat on the bed with his back pressed up against the headboard. I dove into his lap, drawing his semi-erect cock between my lips while stroking the length of it with both hands.

The warm smell of his skin made me feel completely relaxed about what we were going to try, even though the size of his erection was a bit unnerving. The feeling of holding him in my mouth was unbelievably satisfying.

He leaned back, stroking my hair and caressing my shoulders as I sucked him hard, covering him completely with my wet mouth.

"You didn't ask permission, baby. So I owe you a spanking some other time."

I looked up to see him grinning, and fluttered my eyelashes. "Anytime, Master."

"In my lap," he commanded, and I jumped up to straddle him.

I immediately realized where he was going with this, and I was relieved that I would be the one in control of the speed and pressure. He coated his shaft in lube, then brought the thick crown to my tight little asshole.

"Slow and easy, baby," he murmured, cupping my ass gently with one hand. He brought his mouth to mine, but something felt different. He had kissed me hard many times, but this time it felt like he was owning me. Capturing me. Making me his.

I could taste my own tangy flavor on his lips, and it was so erotic I felt myself practically melting. Tensing my thighs carefully, I lowered myself onto his giant cock just an inch. It felt so strange to be opening this part of my body to anything, but I could do anything for my sexy man.

I'd heard people speak of subspace before, but never truly understood what they meant. Now I knew. I was floating outside of my body with no real thoughts, just physical sensations and a warm wave of knowing my Master would take care of me.

Working my hips carefully, I raised and lowered myself a tiny bit so that his thickness was taking small, delicate strokes into my ass. It was incredibly tight, but it didn't hurt.

Working slowly, I felt the head and at least two inches of cock inside me.

"Stop, sweetheart. Take it slow. How does that feel?"

"Mmm," I moaned, pressing my lips to his again as I moved up and down slowly, working him just a millimeter deeper with every gentle thrust.

Feeling him stretch me open like this was intense, but beautiful. I wiggled a bit, trying to keep everything loose, then descended a bit more.

"Emma, that feels so fucking good."

I looked into his eyes and saw that Darren looked almost dizzy with lust.

Gripping my ass in both hands, he held me up, letting me control how much I sunk down on his thickness. Bit by bit I lowered myself, rocking my hips as I wound my arms around his neck.

He tilted me back for a moment, watching his thick shaft enter my tightest hole, watching my body open for him. Then I leaned forward again, angling him deep as I moved lower. We moaned together, rocking gently, completely lost in sensation.

I finally sank down completely, releasing all pressure on my legs so that his entire cock was as deep inside me as it could go.

Looking at him with wide eyes, I giggled. "Wow. It worked."

He chuckled, then murmured, "Just stay still for a minute." We breathed together, still and perfect, then I began moving gently again.

"Emma, you are perfection. Do you understand this?"

"Mmm," I moaned, my thighs tensing gently as I raised and lowered myself slowly on his enormous cock.

"Are you okay, baby? You like this?"

My eyes opened lazily. It was so sweet the way he constantly checked on me. "Yes, Master. This feels wonderful." Gripping his shoulders, I raised myself a bit more, then descended, working his shaft deeper. "Does this feel good for you, Sir? Is your pet pleasing you?"

"Yes, baby," he growled, his lips sucking gently along my collarbone.

"Master, if you ever wanted to bite me, go ahead." He'd given me little nips and teasing nibbles here and there, but I needed him to devour me.

His teeth sunk into my skin just enough to thrill me, to

leave a tiny mark, to make me his. The subtle sting made me quiver with primal lust, and I adored the fire in his eyes.

Reaching into the bedside drawer, he pulled out a tiny wireless bullet vibrator, slipping it gently into my wet pussy. As he set the controller to low, a deep rumbling vibration filled us both.

"Oh, fuck," I moaned, raising up again as I began to fuck myself in the ass with his giant cock.

I couldn't be gentle and tender anymore. I needed to be taken. Owned. "Fuck me deep, Master," I begged. " Feel how open I am for you."

"Oh, baby," he groaned, gripping my ass again with both hands. "I love that you opened your sweet little ass wide for me. You're such a good girl to take my whole cock."

I grinned, delighted by his praise. "I love feeling you inside me completely, Master."

"Is my sweet baby going to come for me?"

I nodded, the vibrations quivering my clit from the inside, making every part of my pussy throb. That might have been enough, but he slipped his thick thumb between us to circle my sensitive nub.

"Come hard, my sweet baby. I want to feel my gorgeous pet lose herself with my cock deep in her hot little ass."

"Yes," I moaned. My hips were rocking me in a deep rhythm, his thickness filling me over and over as his thumb caressed my clit. Gripping his shoulders tightly, my entire body began to tremble.

"Oh… Oh, Master," I moaned, then I crushed my lips to his as my orgasm washed over me, clenching my muscles, clenching my pussy, and causing my ass to convulse around the cock buried so deep inside me.

"Good girl," he groaned, pulling me tight against him as he throbbed inside me. Then he was coming hot and deep, spurting his release, claiming me where no one had before.

"Thank you, Master," I whispered, collapsing onto his chest.

He let me catch my breath, then lifted me carefully, setting me down beside him so that I could snuggle under his arm.

I felt so mellow, so perfect, that I was almost giddy with bliss. Surrendering to Darren completely was heaven on earth.

*** THIRTY DAYS ***

Looking down at the beautiful girl in my arms, I couldn't help but smile. Emma's wavy hair was rumpled, she was flushed, exhausted, and just looked utterly and thoroughly fucked.

"Should I take you to bed, baby?"

"Not yet, Master. Snuggles."

Curling my arms around her, I held her gently but angled her so that I could see her eyes clearly.

"Sweetheart, I know that you so that you intended to stay with me for thirty days, and that's up on Saturday."

Opening her eyes slowly, she looked at me with a carefully blank expression. Smiling down at her, I asked, "Would you like to keep seeing me?"

She grinned, her eyes sparkling. "Yes, Master."

I gave her a kiss on the forehead. "Now baby, I told you that I had a bad break up not too long ago." She nodded, serious again. "So I think maybe it would be best for both of us if we took things a bit slowly." She nodded again, and I was relieved that she was listening quite carefully.

"What if we had our own separate lives during the week, but you came to stay with me on weekends? That way we can take things at an easy pace, have some balance in our lives, but still be together?"

"That's a brilliant idea," she said eagerly. "That way we can still stay in touch with our own friends, have our own lives, then I can be your pet for two whole days."

I kissed her nose. "None of those friends of yours are guys, right?" I asked, arching my eyebrow and pretending to be stern.

Her little giggle rang through the room. "Well, there's my best friend's boyfriend and my old buddy from high school. But they're pretty harmless."

"I'm kidding, baby. I swear I'm not really the jealous

type. But I do want to be in an exclusive relationship with you. What do you think about that?"

She nodded quickly before stretching up to kiss me, firmly pressing her lips to mine as if to seal a promise. When she finally pulled away, she whispered, "Yes, Master. I'm your girl. Only yours."

This remarkable woman was giving herself to me so easily, that I realized I needed to do the right thing, and give her reassurance. I needed her to know that I was serious. Even though I promised I would never say these words again for years, it was true, and she should know.

"Baby, you can probably tell that I'm not the hearts and flowers type, and I don't get mushy very often. But I'm incredibly grateful that you're in my life, Emma, and I love you."

Her eyes grew wide, and her bottom lip trembled twice before she whispered, "I love you too, Darren."

I kissed her gently, caressing her lips against mine delicately while her fingers swept around my shoulders, exploring my skin.

"How about you sleep in my bed tonight, and we can curl up with a movie?"

She nodded eagerly, and the happiness I saw in her eyes was something I would devote myself to re-creating every single time we were together.

"Yes, Master."

***

Find more books in the BDSM Training School series by searching "Lexie Renard" on Amazon.

***

MORE HOT, EROTIC STORIES YOU MAY ENJOY:

Heights of Luxury: Dystopian Future Erotic Romance Novel
The air, the light, the technology, the rules... everything was wildly different 71 Levels up. Ellie only had one goal in life – to provide for her little sister. Decadent bachelors Adam and Ben share everything – their business, and their luxury condo up Level 71. When Adam bought Ellie in the Condo Courtesan Auction, he was surprised that his dark urges were finally triggered, and Ben was shocked to discover it was a girl he'd already seen. Will innocent Ellie be able to keep up with their unusual sensual appetites, while following the new restrictive rules of the higher levels? What will happen when she discovers the little secrets that both Ben and Adam tried to hide? 18+: Many *extremely* vivid, graphic sexual scenes.

The Collar - Series: BDSM Submission Erotica
She has given herself to her Master, who controls her completely. She wears a collar at all times, and at the push of a button, he can make her more aroused, more open, and the perfect toy. These are already her natural desires, so it's easy to fine tune the impulses. His kitten is the perfect subject for his neurology experimentation, and she's eager to try everything... Even things that she never thought she'd try again. BDSM, spanking, bondage, intense sexual and sensual scenes.

Billionaire's Sugar Baby: From Trailer Trash to Sex Pet (5 part series)
Grace was shivering in an alley when she met her Prince Charming. Well, he wasn't a prince, but Cole Hawthorne was so rich and powerful in this city it was practically the same thing. When faced with the decision to go back to her trashy trailer park, or come home with Cole, she decides to take a chance and move up in the world. Being Cole's secret mistress could be the answer to all of her problems, but will she be able to satisfy him?

Basement Sex Doll (Series) Mind Control / Hypnosis Erotica
FH Mansion is a secret place where all of your sexual fantasies can be brought to life. Their stunning array of living sex dolls can be programmed to fulfill absolutely any scenario you can possibly imagine.
Trish donates her body to a secret sex club to earn money for university, and is thrilled ato be used as a sex toy. Carrie is signing her body away for ten months, even though she's shy. Will it bring out her wild, primal self?

My Neighbour's Dungeon - 5 part Series BDSM Submission Romance
What does a girl have to do to get the next door neighbor to spank her? Pretty little Lindsay has lived next to gorgeous older hunk Nick for years, but she just accidentally discovered that he is an S&M Master. Super romantic submission and BDSM exploration!

Nomad's Deal: (Sci-Fi Hot Alien Romance): Romance Novella
When Lily first saw the tall, dark alien strangers on TV, it brought back a
long time fantasy she never thought she'd have a chance of fulfilling. She
signed up for the sensual exploration program immediately, hoping to be
with one of these powerful, strange men, and finally make her dark fantasy
come true. Zale was the most caring, sexy man she'd ever met. It didn't
matter to her that he was a little different, and fought to stay in control of
his new self. Lily finally discovers the man she's been needing all along
wasn't quite a man at all.This might be the first Nomad-Human relationship
on Earth, but sweet love and hot times are universal.

Trapped with Two Firemen: Down & Dirty Horror Erotica
Tina has been hiding in the basement, but has been found by two hot,
hulking firefighters just before sunset. They must be silent together in the
dark, listening for the savage, primitive creatures who hunt them. As they
snuggle together for warmth, their own animal urges cannot be ignored.

The Dare – Auction at the BDSM Dungeon: BDSM Submission Erotica
Sometimes it just takes one little push to make your fantasies a reality. Julia
and her best friend often dare each other into big, life changing challenges.
But now Julia is on the auction block at a charity BDSM fundraiser,
being sold for an evening of fun and games even though she doesn't quite
understand the rules. She'll have to get over her fears to have the time of
her life – letting go completely to be someone's submissive, sensual, sexual
plaything for the evening.

Suddenly His Toy - a Sexy Office Pet Romance BDSM Erotica
The job title is "assistant", but the boss wants MUCH more from her…
Sarah is a new assistant, catching the eye of the CEO who wants to use
her as his sex pet and toy. At first she plays his games because she needs
the money, but suddenly she discovers that she's addicted to him - his
punishments, the rough, hot encounters, and the adrenaline that crashes
through her veins every time she's near him.

Coming Soon...
More hot romance novels, and tons of new erotic short stories!
Outlaw Warrior Soldiers – Sci Fi erotic romance.
X Girls – a sub and her brand new Master infiltrate a secret web network.
LexieRenard.com for details, and get on the email list for treats.

If you enjoy sexy modern romance, search for **The Librarian and the
Rock Star**, available on Kindle, Kindle Unlimited, and in Paperback.

About the Author

Romance, S&M romance, erotic romance, and erotica
writer Lexie Renard is from Toronto, Ontario, and
a sketchy bar or dungeon near you.
Yes, she's actually bisexual and into the BDSM scene.
No, you may not see her wrist cuffs, you naughty thing.
If you like romantic, interesting smut, and a wide variety of
strange stories, search "Lexie Renard" on all ebook sites.
(Some sites allow filthier stories than others.)

Get on the email list for a FREE story, longer previews, and
details of new releases: http://eepurl.com/cP-J_L

www.LexieRenard.com

Want to be a hero to an author you enjoy? Review their work online.
Even if it's a super short review, it really helps increase visibility.
On most sites you can change your name to initials if you'd like
to maintain your privacy.

Thanks for being one of the cool people who still read books!

~ *Lexie xox*

Printed in Great Britain
by Amazon

34623511R00066